"You going to be

She shrugged, her mann
I'm just about to go into
fired—if it doesn't get me killed."

She might think she had him fooled, but Rafe had to wonder, was she really up for this?

"Wish me luck." One corner of her mouth quirked, forming a perfect dimple in her cheek. A dimple he pictured himself softly kissing.

He scowled, worry making it crucial to wipe the look from her face, to make her understand how critical this moment was. Looking across the front seat at her, he said, "This is it, Shannon. This means... everything."

Her eyes softening, she nodded. "I know, Rafe," she said. Laying her hand atop his, she gave him a reassuring squeeze.

He felt her lean over the console an instant before her unexpected kiss lit the powder keg of his confusion. As he turned to wrap an arm around her, to drag her even closer, moist heat exploded, mouth to mouth and man to woman.

But as much as Rafe would have liked to taste, to touch, to break the unbearable tension for a short time, he pushed her away, his brain reminding him of the business at hand and his heart's blood going ice-cold with suspicion.

Is Special Agent Shannon Brandt trying to get me so worked up I won't notice that she's kissing me goodbye?

COLLEEN THOMPSON

CAPTURING THE COMMANDO

TORONTO NEW YORK LONDON
AMSTERDAM PARIS SYDNEY HAMBURG
STOCKHOLM ATHENS TOKYO MILAN MADRID
PRAGUE WARSAW BUDAPEST AUCKLAND

To old friends, lost friends, and fond memories.
Thanks for being part of the journey.

Recycling programs
for this product may
not exist in your area.

ISBN-13: 978-0-373-69553-9

CAPTURING THE COMMANDO

ABOUT THE AUTHOR

After beginning her career writing historical romance novels, Colleen Thompson turned to writing the contemporary romantic suspense she loves in 2004. Since then, her work has been honored with the Texas Gold Award, along with nominations for RITA®, Daphne du Maurier and multiple reviewers' choice honors, along with starred reviews from *RT Book Reviews* and *Publishers Weekly*. A former teacher living with her family in the Houston area, Colleen has a passion for reading, hiking and dog rescue. Visit her online at www.colleen-thompson.com.

Books by Colleen Thompson

HARLEQUIN INTRIGUE
1286—CAPTURING THE COMMANDO

CAST OF CHARACTERS

Shannon Brandt—A rookie FBI field agent with everything to prove, for Shannon, failure's not an option—any more than falling for the man she's sworn to stop at any price.

Rafe Lyons—This decorated Army Ranger will stop at nothing to avenge his little sister's death and find his missing niece—even if that means kidnapping one gorgeous federal agent.

Lyssa Lyons Smith—Murdered in her eighth month of pregnancy, Lyssa had finally moved beyond her troubled youth to find happiness in the months before her death. Or had she?

Garrett Smith—The computer geek is helping Rafe track his wife's killer. But is his grief for Lyssa real or carefully contrived?

Steve Brandt—Though he thinks his sister is better suited for teaching preschoolers than hunting felons, sibling rivalry won't stop this special agent from rescuing Shannon at any cost.

Dominic Powers—This shady lawyer will do anything to keep his luxurious South Florida lifestyle intact—no matter how many must suffer and die to ensure it.

Chapter One

Tampa, Florida
August 21, 7:20 a.m.

He had her dead to rights.

Maybe *dead,* in fact, too, Shannon Brandt realized as a deep voice warned, "Don't move," and something hard jammed into her back. The barrel of a handgun? All from a passerby she'd barely noticed as she hurried to the corner breakfast joint where the rest of her team was already positioned, ready to make the grab. The tall white male, face mostly hidden by the brim of a goofy tourist ball cap, had been looking down, apparently engrossed in a brochure for the kitschy mermaid park nearby. He'd seemed harmlessly distracted, with a diaper bag tucked guy-style, like a football, beneath one arm. Waiting for his wife, she thought, and paying no heed to anyone else.

Or so it had seemed until the moment she'd passed and he was out of sight.

Her stomach plummeted when he ground out, "Into the car. Now. We'll have our little talk there, *Special Agent.*"

Giving her a slight push, he propelled her not toward the nondescript stolen vehicle she might have expected but to a cherry-red Cadillac the size of the *Queen Mary*. The gas-sucking seventies engine rumbled, and she saw a sweaty-looking pale man with dark, reflective glasses slouched low behind the wheel.

Though shaded by a floppy beach hat, the driver's weak chin gave him away as one Garrett Smith, she realized, her heart constricting with the knowledge that that meant the man behind her, the fake dad with the weapon, was well prepared to use it—that he was the very fugitive she'd been so certain she had fooled into walking into their trap.

She blanched, wondering how long it had taken him to figure out she was FBI. And whether he meant to retaliate for her online masquerade and efforts to entrap him.

She sucked in a lungful of humid air, thinking of the slim-frame Glock in her inside waistband holster. But thinking, too, of the half-dozen civilians gathered at the nearby bus stop, the men and women on the sidewalk with their greasy sacks of sugary doughnuts and newspapers, or their lunches packed for a new workday.

For a split second her mind lost its purchase, allowing the memory of another nightmare to crash its way through to reality. The concussive blast, exactly where she'd ordered the tactical team to place its charges. The hot crimson slick spreading from beneath the collapsed wall.

The cigar store hostages in Iowa, whose lives she had been charged with saving. The hostages whose lives she'd blown away just two months ago…

The faint drawl of a West Texas accent yanked her ruthlessly back to the present.

"Make a move for that gun and this goes real bad in a

hurry, Special Agent. I promise you, we're only talking. I swear it as an officer of the U.S. Army Rangers."

"An *AWOL* officer," she corrected, "on a mission your superiors never authorized and—"

"Let's go catch up with your mother, honey," Captain Rafe Lyons interrupted, his deep voice turning cheerful. "The little guy probably needs changing by now."

Adrenaline detonating in hot waves all through her, she couldn't wrap her brain around the shock of this game changer. Around the fact that rather than playing a crucial role in capturing the commando, she was the one being taken to his waiting car instead. Taken captive, possibly—or maybe to be killed before her thirtieth birthday, regardless of what he had just promised.

She could already hear the voices, the old guard bureau veterans at her funeral scoffing, *If that girl was half the agent her old man was, she'd have fought her way free and dragged Lyons back in handcuffs.* Could picture her older brother, Steve, a special agent working out of Oklahoma, wondering aloud why she couldn't quit competing with him and find herself a nice safe job teaching preschool.

Like hell, Steve. Fury ramping past her fear, Shannon pivoted, one hand reaching for her waistband, while the other rose to shove aside her assailant's weapon and allow her enough space to go on the attack.

But though she'd practiced such defense tactics in scores of training sessions, Lyons was no ordinary sparring partner. Dropping his arm beneath her grasp, he closed in and brought his hand—the hand holding what she took to be a pistol—up against her neck. Before she could cry "Rape!" or free her own gun, she felt herself tumbling, glittering blue bursts crackling through her brain and muscles. Independent of her will, her head and limbs flailed wildly with the voltage surging through her.

Not a gun—a stun gun, her mind registered as her body crumpled, her forehead smacking the sidewalk and heat streaking past her eyes. As the jolt ended, she heard the Ranger, with his maddening Texas accent, telling the gathering bystanders, "Stand clear. Police business." She could picture him flashing a wallet with a badge and an official-looking ID.

Though there were a few murmurs, the onlookers scurried away, eager to look elsewhere as he deftly removed her Glock.

A minute later, as Lyons flipped the front seat forward and shoved her into the white leather backseat cavern, Shannon struggled to fight, but her abused muscles would only twitch uselessly in response. He climbed in beside her, and his big hands frisked her briskly and efficiently, plucking the cell phone from the pocket of her khaki skirt and dropping that lifeline— with its built-in GPS—beside the curb.

He reached to close the door and urged the driver, "Let's go."

The man Shannon had ID'd as Lyons's brother-in-law pulled out into traffic. Sped up to take her somewhere that her team, only a block distant, couldn't follow.

She fought to sit up, but her body was having none of it. She struggled to protest, but her words spilled out in an incoherent jumble. Instead, she coughed, choking on the acrid taste of her own terror. Or maybe there was blood, too. Judging from the pain, she'd bitten her tongue, and something was dripping down her forehead, which felt as if she'd cracked it open like an egg.

"Don't try to talk." Bent over her, Lyons briefly came into focus, with his chiseled features, short hair black and shiny as a panther's, and intense green eyes set in a worried face.

He started to cuff Shannon's hands behind her, then appeared to change his mind, binding them in front instead and pressing a towel he pulled out of the diaper bag into them. "Hold this against your forehead." As he spoke, he winced, regret flashing across his handsome features.

She reached up, wiping at the bloody mess and struggling to reorder her scrambled thoughts. When she touched the rising lump with the towel, she groaned and struggled not to be sick, pain slicing like a cleaver through her skull.

"Wish that hadn't had to happen," he said, perspiration rolling down the side of his face. "It shouldn't have been necessary. I told you, I just wanted to talk."

"W-would *you* have bought that and…and gone quietly?" The words sounded thick and clumsy in her ringing ears.

"Well, *no,*" he allowed. "But that's me, and—anyway, I'm not the one sitting here bleeding."

"And I'm not the one heading to Leavenworth for assaulting and abducting a federal officer," she told the man she had already pegged as just another macho cowboy. Having been raised, alongside her chauvinistic brother, in Wyoming by a testosterone-breathing uncle, she was well-acquainted with the breed—and couldn't wait to slap cuffs on this Texas-born example.

As the vintage Cadillac picked up speed and cornered sharply, Shannon would have fallen to the floorboards if Lyons's strong hands hadn't grabbed her.

"Damn it. Careful, Garrett," he barked. "We don't need to draw any more attention."

"You're calling me by *name?*" the driver complained, sounding as nervous as he had every right to be.

Lyons laughed. "You're kidding, right? The agent here knows exactly who we are. As much as she knows anything, in the shape she's in right now."

"You promised me nobody'd get hurt. Nobody but those *murderers*..." Grief choked Garrett's voice to a whimper. "God. *Lissa*..."

With the heel of his hand, Rafe popped the corner of the driver's seat. "Don't say her name. All right? Not now. Not until we find them. Then we can ram it down their throats."

Lissa Lyons Smith, they meant. Garrett's wife of two years and Rafe Lyons's little sister. The sister he had raised after their parents' deaths in a head-on collision, when Lissa had been fourteen to her brother's twenty-two.

The same sister who had been brutally murdered almost exactly ten years later. Only three weeks ago in Abilene, she'd been found, her eight-months-pregnant body an empty husk. The medical examiner had determined she'd already been dead, or at least deeply unconscious, from the shattering blow to her skull before the killers started cutting.

Shannon prayed that part was true. But whether or not it was, the young woman's death and her child's disappearance had been more than enough to bring the Ranger captain known by his men as "the Lion" back early from his combat mission in Afghanistan.

It had been more than enough, too, to send the decorated Ranger—by all accounts, a hero—AWOL following the funeral. Out of reach and out of control as he pursued a mission—a personal vendetta—of his own...

One he had begun by punching out the lead Amarillo detective in frustration before returning to his home base in Georgia, closing out his bank accounts and emptying his gun case.

"You don't—you don't need to do this. We want… We're working to find them, too," Shannon explained, though waves of pain like black tar were rolling across her vision. *Whatever you do,* she told herself, *you can't pass out.*

Would they dump her somewhere if she did? Maybe even kill her? Or did Lyons mean to kill her anyway, as a warning to back off, directed at the team assembled to rein in one maverick the government deemed too valuable—or too dangerous—to allow to run amok?

"Those animals are strictly secondary targets." Lyons's anger only intensified the pounding inside her head. "I'm working to find *her.*"

"Her…?" Who did he mean?

On that fateful evening, neighborhood witnesses had spotted a white plumbing van leaving the Smiths' home—a vehicle found abandoned only hours later, not far from where a Ford SUV had been taken from the garage of a vacationing neighbor. When the theft was finally reported three days later, the vehicle's anti-theft tracking system located it abandoned in Northern Florida—less than a mile off of I-10, the main east-west corridor that ran across the Southern U.S.

There were a host of theories, each more horrifying than the last, regarding the crime itself, but state and federal investigators alike agreed on one fact. The two assailants had been male, with both sporting facial hair and a compact, muscular build.

It seemed likely the men were working for someone else, a monster who had set all this in motion. Could a creature cruel enough to order an unborn infant sliced from the womb of an expectant mother possibly be a woman?

The light in Rafe's green eyes went almost feral. "My niece. I only want my niece back."

"Of course." She cursed her spinning head and the confusion that came with it. "Then you've found evidence the baby survived?"

"We were going to have a girl." Smith's voice broke as he interrupted. "A little girl, and we were going to name her Amber Lee."

"But do you know the baby lived?" Gritting her teeth against the pain, Shannon focused on the question, on keeping her eyes open.

"We don't have hard proof," Smith admitted. "But we think… She *has* to—"

"She's alive," Rafe promised, his voice a rumble of barely suppressed emotion. "She's alive, and I'll kill anyone who stands between me and getting that little girl back to her family."

Dabbing once more at the dripping blood, Shannon pushed herself into a sitting position, then stared up at him and challenged, "Does that include a federal agent, Lyons? Because I mean to stop you. I plan to bring you in. Today."

RAFE STARED, dumbfounded, into the brunette's ice-blue eyes. Eyes that stood out starkly from a face that he thought might be attractive despite the blood dripping from the rising purple lump below her hairline.

She was serious, he realized, recognizing the same raw determination that marked the soldiers of his unit. The men who earned the Ranger tab, who earned respect through leadership and combat.

She might have frozen on that crowded street, hesitated for the single instant it took him to predict what she would do. But he knew damned well she would have shot any man who was a fraction of a second slower—or any less desperate than he was to find his niece.

Yet it was neither the coldness of her gaze nor the memory of her training that reminded him to tread carefully around her. It was the starkness of her statement, a statement another man might have laughed off but he instead took as a warning.

She would not go quietly. Would not concede defeat even as she slumped back against the plush white leather, her blue eyes fluttering closed.

As Garrett slowed for a red light, a jacked-up black pickup pulled beside them, its bass thumping out a salsa rhythm. Ignoring it, Lyons pushed the towel she'd dropped into her hands, and in that single moment she erupted into action.

She drew back her legs, then screamed and kicked at the driver's-side window, clearly hoping to draw attention, maybe even smash the glass. Still too weak to be effectual, she did no better than a couple of hard thumps.

In less time than it took for Garrett to let out a startled oath, Rafe hauled her around and pushed the fist-size black stun gun against the curve of her waist.

When she went still, he laid on the Texas drawl. "You don't want another friendly zap, now do you? Come on, sugar. Calm down."

Pressing her back against the door, she glared up at him, her look pure poison. But the effort must have cost her, for the face behind the bloody mask paled, and her eyelids fluttered even harder.

Blinking hard, she grimaced and then slurred, "I'm not your 'sugar,' cowboy."

"And I'm not your 'cowboy,' Special Agent," Rafe said with a shake of his head. As the car once more began moving, he said quietly, "But I'd like to be... Well, I sincerely hope to be your *partner* for a while."

First confusion and then mutiny flashed across her face. Her lips moved—he thought he might have read *Hell, no*—but no sound followed.

And wouldn't, as her last measure of determination winked out and those striking blue eyes rolled back into her head.

Chapter Two

Rafe had been wrong, he realized, as he washed her face with the towel Garrett had dampened in the restroom of a gas station. The woman they had taken was nothing like attractive beneath the drying blood. She was *gorgeous,* plain and simple. Maybe not a conventional beauty, with her mouth a little too wide, her brows a bit too dark and her nose tipped upward a bit too much at the end, but taken together with those probing light blue eyes he'd seen, the effect was...damned uncomfortable.

So he shoved the thought out of his brain, ignoring the subtle curves of her toned body and the fact that he'd been without a woman for so long he couldn't—

Guilt burned as if he'd swallowed one of his sergeant's lit cigars. What the hell was his problem, that he could forget Lissa—murdered, mutilated—and lose his focus on her stolen child for even an instant? As a battle-hardened Ranger, he was well trained, experienced at ignoring his body's demands. Hunger, thirst, exhaustion—wasn't he always telling his men these were nothing compared to a warrior's force of will?

As beautiful, as vulnerable, as Special Agent Shannon Brandt might be, he needed to see her only as an asset to be recruited, assuming he could find some way to convince her to cooperate with his plan.

And if the concussion she had clearly sustained wasn't serious enough to drop her into a coma, or maybe even kill her.

As they continued driving south, he pointed out an exit. "That's the one. You need to take that one."

"I've got it—got it." Garrett darted a nervous scowl over his shoulder. "You know, Rafe, you're even *more* annoying when you're a backseat driver."

"You don't have to like me, buddy." Rafe smiled without a trace of humor, thinking that his computer geek brother-in-law wouldn't last a day in infantry. "Just keep in mind that I'm in charge here—and you're my prisoner in all this—every bit as much as she is. You be sure and tell the cops and feds that."

SHANNON PEERED through slitted eyes, then started at the unexpected dimness. Though she felt the movement of a vehicle, it was different, no longer the vintage Caddy with its white-leather backseat.

Sometime during the day she had been moved, strapped into the dark gray cloth rear seat of a completely different vehicle. She sat up and then hissed through clenched teeth as her headache reignited.

"Feeling any better, Special Agent?" Rafe Lyons turned in the front passenger seat to look her over. "You look better. Color's improved."

"Thanks, Nurse Ratched," she said, and raised her cuffed hands to pinch the bridge of her nose. "Nice to know you care."

"Good to see your sense of humor's intact." A wry grin tipped his mouth—a mouth that under different circumstances she might think of as sensual.

"You're mistaken. I'm not laughing, cowboy. What time is it? Where are we?"

"You've been in and out of it all day," he said. "You remember anything?"

Vague snippets crossed her bruised synapses. The droning hum of a highway. Wisps of quiet conversation. A stop someplace—a small house?—where an older woman's sympathetic face floated into view as she helped Shannon change her bloody top. She saw Rafe's face, too, hard-set with concentration as he placed a bandage on her forehead and fed her what he had claimed was a mild painkiller, then helped her to wash it down with bottled water.

Had there been a sleeping pill, too, despite the risks of mixing one with her head injury? Probably not, Shannon decided, recalling the sleepless nights she'd spent in anticipation of the meeting she had set up with Lyons online—a meeting where she'd planned to continue her bureau-sanctioned role as a disaffected girlfriend offering information on his sister's killers. The biggest operation she had taken part in since the hostage debacle in Iowa, Rafe Lyons's capture was perhaps her final chance to prove she was fit for duty.

Suppressing a groan at the thought of how she'd blown it, she forced herself to say, "I remember stopping someplace. There was an older couple, I think. Someone helping you…"

"I forced them," Rafe was quick to claim. "Just like I'm forcing you and Garrett. I'm the only one here in violation of the law."

Instantly she understood that he was protecting his accomplices from the consequences of their actions. Shielding his brother-in-law, especially, so Garrett Smith would keep his freedom. Would be around to raise his child.

Considering the questions his wife's murder investigation had brought up, Shannon wasn't sure the man deserved the Ranger's sacrifice. Nonetheless, she promised, "You let me go right now and that's what I'll tell everyone."

She didn't really care about punishing the older couple—whom she suspected were retired military—for helping the Ranger. And if her suspicions about Garrett Smith proved true and Rafe learned of them, Lyons would probably kill his brother-in-law with his bare hands.

Ignoring her offer, Rafe said, "It's just about eight-thirty. We should make the motel anytime now. Then we'd better grab some dinner. You must be hun—"

Eight-thirty? Her head spun as she considered the sheer number of lost hours, underscored by the fading summer sky and the dim silhouettes of trees along the roadside. Heart rate ratcheting skyward, she demanded once more, "Where have you taken me?"

In the more than twelve hours since her capture, they could have crossed state lines twice or even three times. Though she knew they'd made at least one stop, she had no idea how long they had stayed off the roads—or how they could have possibly avoided what must have been a massive law enforcement effort to locate and rescue her.

In the distance she saw lights, the dark towers of buildings stacked before a gray-blue blur. The ocean? Gulf? Could this mean they were still somewhere in Florida?

"Little beach community, not too far from Palm

Beach," he said, confirming her suspicion. "Think of this as a vacation."

"Real funny," she shot back. "And here I'd pegged you for a cowboy, not a clown."

"I'm neither," Rafe said roughly. "Just a man looking to find out what happened to the only blood family he has left on this planet—and why someone would butcher my little sister like she was nothing. No one."

Empathy stirred Shannon's heart as she heard the desperate grief behind his anger. Enough grief and desperation to throw away his career, his very freedom, to save his sister's child.

"You could drop this right now," Shannon said. "Before somebody really gets hurt. People—even your superiors—aren't without compassion for your situation, and you can bet the FBI and more local agencies than you can shake a stick at are all committed to the search for your niece and your sister's killers. If you'll let me, Lyons—*Rafe*—I could get you a good deal, maybe even keep you out of prison so you can see that baby when we find her. Be the kind of uncle she can count on to help raise her."

If we find her alive. Though the pair believed to have murdered Lissa Smith was suspected in other similar crimes, none of the missing babies had ever been recovered, and the purpose of their abduction remained a mystery. Black-market trafficking? Blood rituals? The possibilities were endless, each one more sickening than the last.

"Listen to her, Rafe," Garrett urged, a note of pleading in his voice. "It can't hurt to listen to what she says."

The vehicle, which she'd decided was a midsize SUV of some sort, slowed to make a left turn beside a faded sign that read The Seashell Motel—Your Home Away from Home Since 1957. Behind it lay a long one-story structure, a single bar of back-to-back rooms squatting on the far side of a tiny, ill-lit pool. A very few vehicles, all of them older models, offered evidence that this mom-and-pop enterprise was barely clinging to life—a far cry from the luxury hotels she would have expected in this area.

"I have no intention of listening to a word of Agent Brandt's *deal*," Rafe said firmly, clearly used to pulling rank on others. "I brought her here for one reason and one reason only. To talk her into *mine*."

"What about your career?" According to Shannon's research, the thirty-two-year-old had little else. No steady girlfriend, no other family, and few friends beyond the members of his tight-knit Ranger unit, which had its home base in Georgia. Other than the accent, he'd left behind his West Texas past, including the rodeo bull riding circuit, where he'd competed in his youth.

He was one cowboy who'd traded in his hat—along with his heart and soul and loyalty—for a U.S. Army Ranger beret and the unique camaraderie of Special Operations.

Desperate to leverage that bond, she added, "Those Rangers—they're your family, too, right? You're just going to bail on them in wartime?"

His green eyes glared back at her. "You'd better think about your *own* career, sugar. Because from what I've learned about that hostage standoff back in Iowa, you're about one screwup short of being booted from the only job that's ever mattered to you…Daddy's girl."

She blinked back angry tears that she would never dare shed. They blurred Lyons's outline, smudging his dark navy T-shirt and the hard planes of his face.

"Go straight to hell," she murmured, her sympathy for his motives vaporizing in the white heat of her reaction to his cruelty.

SHANNON WAS STILL SEETHING when Rafe finally ordered her into the room. Garrett had checked them into an end unit, a room decorated with cheesy paintings of the beach and a peeling seashell wallpaper border, though any view of the Atlantic had long since been obstructed by the newer oceanfront hotels.

"I'm headed out to pick up dinner," Garrett told them. "Anything you two want?"

Shannon thrust her shackled wrists toward his face. "How 'bout something with a file baked inside it? Or better yet, a working cell phone?"

Rafe shot her an annoyed look from where he was unplugging the second of two grimy-looking rotary phones. "Lock these in the Jeep, will you, Garrett? No need to tempt the agent. And as far as food, it's just fuel, that's all. So pick whatever you like."

Garrett pulled off his beach hat and raked his fingers through limp, sandy-blond hair. About five-ten and still a little on the pale side, he was nonetheless a decent-looking specimen. Squeamish, though, in contrast to the Ranger. Regardless of her suspicions, Shannon tried to appeal to his softer nature.

"I could really use some aspirin or something, anything extra-strength to help knock back this headache." Though that was true enough, she feigned exhaustion as she dropped into one of the old oak chairs and put her feet up on one of two sagging full-sized beds. "And maybe...if it wouldn't be too much trouble, a box of tampons—super plus?"

That part was pure fiction, but she had never met the man who would dare to call a woman on the bluff.

"Um…" Garrett's gray-eyed gaze slid toward Rafe, as if for help. When none was forthcoming, he finally shrugged and murmured, "Sure, I guess so," before slinking out to escape while he could.

"You're good. I'll give you that," Rafe allowed as he stepped up to the door and hooked the security chain. "But don't count on playing on his sympathies and turning him against me."

Stalking back to where she sat, he looked like a mountain of pure, male muscle—six feet three inches, and two-hundred-ten pounds' worth, according to his records.

Refusing to be intimidated, Shannon fixed him with a fierce look, daring him to come one step nearer. "And don't count on getting my help by throwing my past up in my face. You don't win friends with bludgeons— or is brute force all they taught you back in Ranger school?"

He grimaced, and a long sigh followed. "Sorry, Agent. I know better. But that shot about me abandoning my men in wartime—that was way over the line. They're family, too, to me."

"Then let's agree. Family's off-limits. Especially *mine*." And most especially the father she had lost at age eight, the father she and her brother had both been raised to revere, with his every artifact an idol in their rancher uncle's house. Her stomach shrank down to a red-hot coal as Rafe's *Daddy's girl* crack echoed through her memory.

"Got it." He stuck out his right hand, offering to shake.

Ignoring it, she added, "And if you ever dare to bring up Iowa again, I swear to you that one way or another, I *will* find a way to burn you. You can count on it."

To his credit, he didn't smile or remind her that she was the one in handcuffs but simply nodded. "You've got yourself a deal, Brandt."

"Good. Then right now, you have my undivided attention. Tell me about this plan of yours."

"All right, then." He moved his bulky duffel bag to the closet alcove next to the small bathroom, then sat in the chair beside hers.

"Okay," he said. "The way I figure it, you can come out of this one of two ways. The inept, helpless victim—"

"Enough with the flattery," she said with a scowl.

"Or the hero," he finished. "The agent who managed to solve a crime and save a child your colleagues couldn't, all on your own."

"I'm liking that part," she admitted, imaging herself turning the tables in the process and marching the handsome fugitive in at gunpoint. As her fantasy unfolded, her big brother—who would almost certainly have come to Florida by this time—would stand up and lead the round of applause. "How 'bout we dispense with the cuffs and get right to it?"

His forehead creased in either surprise or amusement. "I'm sure you'd enjoy that. But first, I need your agreement that you mean to help…with the best cause that there is."

"Let me guess," she ventured. "It's finding Lissa's baby."

As he shook his head, a fierce light gleamed behind his deep green eyes. "Not just finding her daughter. Finding and returning *all* the stolen babies. All the infants a man named Dominic Powers has ordered torn from their dying mothers and then sold to the highest bidder to fund his personal empire."

Chapter Three

He saw on her face that she didn't know the name. That in spite of the dozens of investigators working in the five states where women had been murdered, Garrett's hacker sources, with their willingness to use extralegal means, had uncovered a connection that law enforcement hadn't found—if the feds even knew they were looking at a serial case. Rafe still wasn't sure exactly how they'd pinpointed Powers, but his sources had come up with enough corroborating evidence to convince him that the unscrupulous attorney was their man.

"How many do you think you're looking at?" she asked, her eyes giving away nothing.

"There have been five that we know of," he said. "Five similar murders of last-trimester pregnant women."

"We've come up with eight," she said. "Most of them in the Gulf Coastal states, though your sister's death was the only one as far west as Texas. My partner calls them the Madonna Murders—though we've managed to keep that away from the press so far, to avoid mass hysteria."

"People have the right to know." Anger speared through him. Lissa might not have had to die if the feds had been willing to alert the public. "They have the right to protect themselves and their loved ones."

"It's a delicate balance," Shannon admitted, "but that decision came from way above my pay grade."

"That's no excuse," he murmured.

"We've learned that men driving stolen white vans marked with the names of fictitious plumbing companies were seen leaving at least three of the scenes. But Dominic Powers—that's a new name to me. What can you tell me about him?"

"Forty-six years old, Caucasian. Currently renting a thirteen-point-six-million-dollar villa right down the road in Palm Beach after twenty years in Houston."

Her lips parted as her brows rose. "Thirteen-point-six?"

He nodded to confirm what he and Garrett had discovered from the tax rolls. "Married three times," Rafe continued. "The most recent spouse filed for divorce and pressed charges for domestic battery. Wife number two vanished a few years prior. Powers claims she ran off with a boyfriend, while her family swears she'd never leave, much less stay away, without a word to them."

"How'd number one get off so easy?"

Rafe shook his head, then shrugged. "We weren't able to find any trace, so for all we know, she's stuffed in a barrel somewhere offshore."

Shaking her head, Shannon blew out a long breath. "So how'd this charmer end up in the black-market baby business? I don't suppose it was his compassion for childless families."

"His passion for the good life is more like it. He tended to pick wives with money and made sure a good chunk of it stayed with him, even when they didn't."

"Tends to happen that way when the spouse takes off for parts unknown. Or conveniently drops dead."

Rafe nodded. "He seems to like the trappings. Flashy

women, flashy lifestyle. Speedboats, sports cars, prestige ZIP codes—a hell of a lot more than he could afford on what he made as a family law attorney back in Texas. Maybe it turned out to be even more than he could fund with the occasional disappearing rich wife."

"Family law…" In spite of what she'd been through and how she must be feeling, Shannon's gaze was focused, her expression razor-sharp. "So he would have dealt with adoption cases back in Houston, right?"

"He had an office on the edge of River Oaks," Rafe confirmed. "So I imagine he saw plenty of wealthy families desperate for a shortcut to claiming a healthy, white newborn they could call their own. And very, very grateful when he could make their dreams come true, no matter how he did it."

"Then at some point a lightbulb comes on…" Shannon's handcuffs jingled as she snapped her fingers "…and Powers decides he's looking at an unmet, extremely strong consumer demand. And who is he to deny the market?"

"He's a dead man, that's who he is," Rafe vowed as he thought of Lissa, the pounding of his own pulse a war drum in his ears. The need for vengeance roared past the grief that had ripped him open. His heart had gone missing, along with his capacity for mercy.

"I thought you were only out to save your niece," Shannon countered, but the words had no heat in them. And her slight smile said she understood, hinted that she wouldn't argue with any outcome that left Powers and his men dead—or at least she wouldn't protest too stringently. "Your niece and those other babies."

"If I have to choose between revenge and getting them out," he said, "I won't have to think about my decision for a second. But if I get my shot at Powers or those butchers he sent for my sister…"

"A man could be forgiven for taking whatever measures necessary to free a captive family member, or even other innocents," Shannon advised him, "but when it comes to a cold-blooded revenge killing, all bets are off, Captain. You know that as well as I do."

Rafe drew a deep breath to clear his head, then answered, "I'm not a man looking for forgiveness. I've come way too far to give a damn about that. All I care about is making this work. After that, the Army, the FBI, the cops—they can all pick at my bones or whatever else is left of me."

She had no answer except to look at him, her gaze as reproachful as it was somber. Could she—the same woman he'd shocked and abducted—be feeling some measure of compassion for him, along with the victims of Powers's crimes?

Rafe didn't need and certainly didn't want her pity, so he hurried to fill the space with an explanation of the operation he had come up with, a raid that would stand only a ghost of a chance—and then only if she would agree to help him.

Shannon leaned forward, listening intently, her blue eyes lasering straight through his bravado to focus on the risks inherent in the plan.

When he had finished, she shook her head. "That's crazy. You know that, don't you? Why not just let the feds conduct the raid? We have the people and the training. We can assemble…" A shadow passed over her beautiful features, troubling her expression. "We can… I can order the tactical teams and SWAT departments to breach those walls and get—inside."

When she paled, he suspected she was thinking of

the Iowa cigar store standoff he'd researched online after Garrett had determined his "informant's" true identity. He saw in her eyes that she was haunted by the two women and the new father who had died in the wake of her miscalculation. An error based on the best intelligence she'd had at the time.

From his own experience in combat, he knew civilians sometimes became casualties despite every effort to minimize that risk. He recognized, too, the look of PTSD, the post-traumatic stress disorder he saw written in her blue eyes.

But he pretended not to see it, respecting his promise not to bring up the incident. Instead he zeroed in on his real concern. "What do you think the odds are of the feds taking my information—data illegally obtained by Garrett's hacker buddies—as gospel and running with it before another woman dies?"

"We'd make it top priority, but you're right, there would have to be independent, legally obtained confirmation. For the search warrant, among other things—"

"And," he added, "you'd also have a hell of a lot of interdepartmental chest-thumping as all the various bureaucracies fought for jurisdiction and wrangled over who got to take the credit."

She opened her mouth as if to argue, then very slowly let it close before nodding. "Even if I *were* crazy enough to agree to take part in this lunacy," she began, "do you honestly think a force of three has a prayer of pulling this off without getting a bunch of people killed? Starting with us, I mean."

"I've come back from riskier missions," he told her. "And run more than a few of 'em myself."

"With men you trusted?"

"With my life."

"Yeah, well, this time," she said, "you'd have exactly two on your team. A woman whose career is toast if she doesn't betray you, and a techno-nerd brother-in-law who—no offense—looks like he couldn't fight his way out of buying siding from a determined telemarketer. Do you really imagine you can rely on us?"

"It's a chance I'm willing to take."

"For what, Rafe? Because I can't begin to imagine that a guy like Dominic Powers is keeping a bunch of infants stockpiled at his swanky Palm Beach *hacienda*. Can you?"

"There'll be records of where they've gone. Who's adopted those kids. Somewhere. I have a source that mentioned some kind of ledger he keeps close at hand. He takes it out of his wall safe every morning."

"And you think it's his client list, maybe even records related to the babies' mothers?"

"That's exactly what we're hoping."

"Is that another risk you're willing to take? There sure seem to be a lot of them."

"I'll find some way to do this," he swore through gritted teeth. "With or without your help."

She shook her head. "You're not the only one who knows a bluff when she hears one. You wouldn't have risked snatching me off a crowded street if you thought you had a shot without me. But before you risk both our lives on some half-baked raid against what you and I both know will be a well-fortified, heavily guarded compound, there's something you should know. Some information *I* have that your amateur-hour investigation didn't turn up."

Though he bristled at being called an amateur—especially considering how he'd caught her off-guard earlier that day—Rafe clamped his jaw shut to hear out what she had to say.

Would it be another lie, like those she'd spun online in her bid to snare him, or was it possible she might be seriously considering helping him?

TIME TO TREAD CAREFULLY, Shannon warned herself as apprehension knotted in the hollow of her stomach.

Nothing she did, nothing she said, during this crisis could be more dangerous than the news she had to give him. Unwelcome news that might easily spark the ugliest of reactions in a man who had already crossed so many lines.

But however many laws he had shattered, however many oaths and regulations he had sacrificed, she still sensed a core of honor in him. A set of rigid values he placed above all bureaucratic rules.

Here's hoping that not punching a woman is part of that code. After reinforcing her courage with a deep breath, she lobbed her opening volley. "It's about your sister's husband, Garrett."

Rafe snorted in disgust, contempt written in his green eyes. "Don't tell me you're going to try that divide-and-conquer bullshit on me, too."

She leaned slightly forward, determined to cut through his distrust. "Listen to me, Lyons. Your brother-in-law... We think he's had a girlfriend, a lover, these past six months. A woman he met online and—"

When Rafe jumped to his feet, she jerked back, then cursed herself for reacting. For showing she'd been physically intimidated, when all he was doing was getting up to pace the room.

Yet she couldn't force herself to relax, for there was nothing safe about the wild energy crackling through his muscles, or the warning, low as a growl, in his voice when he spoke.

"Don't you dare sit there and try to play me," he said. "Don't imagine for a minute I'm that stupid."

She sat back, scarcely breathing, waiting for his anger to wind down. But he was only getting started, his temper revving to the red zone.

"Do you know Garrett was the one who found her?" Rafe demanded. "Can you imagine what it did to him, a guy like that, who's worked in nice clean offices his whole life and doesn't even like to think about where his chicken dinners come from, walking into that *hell* he saw? I've seen some horrible things in war zones, but the idea of what he found that night—Lissa left—left like some animal had torn into her…"

He swallowed audibly, his voice choking down to silence, the silence that so often marked the helpless rage of the survivor of a loved one's murder. Seeing it, Shannon was haunted by the echo of her own pain, her impotent eight-year-old fury, after her father was gunned down.

If she had been a grown woman when it happened, a woman qualified to fire automatic weapons and trained to deliver a crushing blow to a man's most vulnerable targets, would she have taken the law into her own hands as Rafe was doing now? If she had had a chance to save some part of her father, would she have been willing to sacrifice anything she had, even her own life, as Rafe would to reclaim Lissa's daughter?

"Listen, Special Agent," Rafe said grimly, "you haven't lived with Garrett these past two weeks, haven't heard the way he wakes up screaming about the blood. You haven't watched the guy break down and sob her name, listened to him retching in the bathroom. It's killing him, killing both of us to think of—"

"People feel remorse." Shannon's voice floated to earth as cautiously as the feathery pink seed of a mimosa. "People can feel regret when they're faced with the consequences of what they've set in motion."

He spun around and crossed the room in two steps before grabbing her by the arms with hands as hard as vises. "Not Garrett. I *know* him, know him well enough to trust him to take care of the most important person in my life. And now you have the freaking nerve to accuse him, and you think I'm going to stand here and listen to you do it?"

Heart leaping in her chest, Shannon could do no more than stiffen, frozen by the knowledge that she might have pushed too hard. Might have assumed too much about who this desperate man was, and what he would or wouldn't do to her, despite his need for her cooperation.

He could kill her with his bare hands for the insult she had offered. Almost worse in her mind, he could try to break her will. Considering both his training and the places where his missions had taken him, he would be well acquainted with dozens of methods of coercion, from beatings that wouldn't show to the kind of torture that would scar her soul forever.

Not him. He could never…

Yet despite her efforts to convince herself, she could feel her body recoiling, could hear the trembling of her own exhalation. Her head throbbed with the effort of containing boundless terror.

My father didn't show fear, not even when that drug lord shoved the muzzle underneath his jaw. And my brother wouldn't, either, so I'll be damned if I will, no matter what he does.

The Ranger let go of her and looked away, then resumed his pacing.

To prove she wouldn't be cowed, she forced herself to speak again, to swallow past the hard lump in her throat. "There's more, Rafe. More we found during our investigation."

"Haven't you figured it out yet?" he asked. "I damned well don't want to hear this."

"If you don't want to hear it, then you'd better gag me." She shrugged, struggling to look as though she couldn't care less. To look like a strong woman in a tough spot, rather than the quivering mass of nerves she felt like behind the mask. "Though you'll have to admit, that would probably put a damper on the team-building aspect of this operation. Even more, I think, than leaving a goose egg on my forehead or these bruises on my arms."

His gaze flicked to the reddened fingerprints on her forearms, and a troubled look passed over his face. Raking his hand through his black hair, he shook his head and said, "Fine, then. Say whatever it is you think you have to tell me. I won't promise to listen—but you don't have to worry that I'll hurt you for it."

Shannon wouldn't bet her life on that, then realized that in a way, she did with her next words. "The weekend before Lissa's murder, Garrett played golf with his neighbor. The same neighbor who mentioned he was about to fly to California with his family, leaving his Ford Explorer locked up in the garage."

Rafe stared at her, the color draining from his face. "The same SUV the killers stole and drove to Florida? You're telling me that this guy told him about it?"

Relieved beyond measure that something she had said had sunk in, Shannon nodded. "Garrett knew," she said. "Knew it would take days for the theft to be discovered. And more than that, his neighbor gave him a spare house key and asked Garrett to bring in a package he was expecting."

"Which would've given him access to the garage."

"I have the man's sworn statement. When the family came home, they discovered the SUV keys missing from the kitchen counter where he'd left them. But nothing else was taken, nothing but that Ford Explorer."

Speculation narrowed Rafe's eyes before he turned his suspicious gaze on her. "So that's it? That's all you have? A little online flirtation and some neighbor dumb enough to leave his keys in plain sight of a window? And if he told Garrett he was going, who else might have known? Or mentioned it to their friends?"

She nodded, deciding to hold off for now on telling him about the hotel receipts that put Garrett Smith's affair well beyond the level of flirtation and try a new tack. "We were also concerned about his ties to online hackers."

Rafe shrugged it off. "Sometimes he recruits them to test their skills against a database or a network he's securing. Bomb-proofing his security work with a little friendly fire makes a lot of sense to me. Besides, those hackers are the ones who've helped us put everything together. They might also be the key to finding those babies and the people who paid big bucks to adopt them."

Shannon wondered how many of the parents knew the true facts behind the adoptions they were paying for in the form of exorbitant fees. And how many hearts would shatter when the hideous truth unfolded. Yet she couldn't let that be her worry, not with so many families desperate to find their stolen children, children who were the last, most sacred legacies of the women who'd been lost.

"You haven't given me a shred of proof that Garrett's involved," said Rafe. "You're only tossing pebbles at a window—distracting me enough to get me worrying about him. Of course, that's the way I would've played it, too. More subtle like that, don't you think? Better to work the wedge of doubt in slowly, instead of pounding it so hard it shatters."

Shannon blew an impatient breath through pursed lips. Of course it couldn't be easy. Not with Rafe so aware of her desperation to derail him, to bring him in to save her career. And maybe their lives, too, because she had seen enough to know that in an operation, almost anything could happen. Including outcomes no one involved intended. "Just think about it. That's all I ask. Pay attention to how he acts, to anything that doesn't feel right."

This time, when Rafe narrowed his eyes, there was nothing fleeting about his suspicion. "You *are* good, Special Agent Brandt. You're damned good. But you've got one huge shortcoming in this situation."

"You mean *other* than the handcuffs, stun gun, weapons, and huge height and weight advantages you've got on me?" she asked sarcastically, her headache flaring as she rolled her eyes.

This time, when he reached toward her, his touch was gentle, almost playful, as he flicked his callused fingertips beneath her chin. "Your main problem is, I'm better. And I've been two steps ahead of you from the very start."

Chapter Four

Shannon's unruffled demeanor impressed the hell out of Rafe. She was either almost unbelievably cool under pressure or the finest actress he had ever met.

"How 'bout unlocking these cuffs now?" she asked him. "It's darned awkward, using the restroom, and besides, I'd really like to catch a shower if I could."

"A shower," he echoed flatly. "With everything that's going on, you're thinking about soap and water and fluffy towels?"

Her smile hinted that, as with everything else she'd said and done since awakening, this new ploy had its purpose. "Fluffy towels? In this place? If that happened, it would be the second-biggest surprise of my day so far."

"If you're thinking of escaping, you should know that the bathroom has no windows," he warned. "And if you're thinking about potential weapons, I'll be searching you before I let you out. Thoroughly."

She stood and approached him, her shackled hands raised and her palms turned up as if in supplication. But there was nothing pleading in her eyes, only the glint of mild amusement. Maddening amusement, just short of mockery.

Or was it something else? Was she coming on to him

now? Thinking to seduce her way out of this? Trying to get him worked up with the thought of her tight curves beneath the sluicing water—lathered, naked and hotter than the tropical late-summer night?

He nearly groaned aloud at his body's immediate reaction. Damn her anyway, for trotting out this tactic. Why couldn't she stick with something simple, like attempting to claw his eyes out or kick every woman's favorite target up through the roof of his mouth? Those threats, he was equipped to deal with, just as he had been with her attempt to poison his mind against Garrett.

"I promise, I'm not thinking of anything but rinsing the dried blood out of my hair and the grit off of my skin," she said innocently.

As if he bought *that* act for a second.

Confirming his suspicions, she added, "I'm also thinking we could have a long wait for your friend Garrett to come back. A *very* long wait…*if* he ever comes back at all."

"He'll be back, all right, though I'm thinking it might take him a while to work up the nerve to make your little *purchase*." Rafe emphasized the word to show her that he didn't buy that tampon story for a second.

Reaching into his pocket, he pulled out a handcuff key. Unable to resist the temptation to see how far she was willing to take this latest attempt to distract him, he lifted the key toward her face and leaned in to whisper, "If I unlock those cuffs, how do I know you'll be good?"

She didn't step back—didn't yield an inch—only looked up into his face through beautiful, long lashes, a knowing smile playing on her full lips. But to his surprise, her voice gave away a nervous tremor as she whispered, "Are you sure you really want me...to be *good?*"

It zinged through his awareness—how close they were standing and how very few steps it would take to sweep her to the bed beneath him. As a distraction, Rafe tried mentally running through the alphabet in reverse. To his infinite annoyance, his thoughts couldn't make it past the letter *x*.

As in X-rated. *Damn it.* How was he supposed to stay two steps ahead of her when he was thinking with his...

"Yes," he managed to say, sliding his key into the tiny lock, turning it slowly and feeling the click of a steel cuff disengaging. His gaze lingered on her pale wrist, on the reddened indentation, the slight bruising, and the way her skin had chafed beneath the metal.

Yet another injury his actions had inflicted on her.

Before he could stop himself, he stroked his thumb across the subtle damage gently, an attempt to rub the sting from her impossibly soft flesh.

"No," she said sharply, her gaze dropping as she turned away and shook her head. "I'm sorry... I can't—I just can't do this."

Rafe felt the perspiration beading on his forehead, felt the burn of shame that made him want to crank the room's noisy AC down to glacial. Laying a palm atop her shoulder, he gave her what he hoped would pass for a sympathetic squeeze. "I'd be disappointed in you if you could. And more disappointed in myself if I weren't Ranger enough to control my..."

Control what? His attraction? Because it was definitely more than simple lust that he was feeling. It was the perfect storm of his awareness of her body, his appreciation of the intelligence sparkling in her blue eyes, and his growing admiration for the way she was handling herself in one hell of a tough situation.

"Control *myself*," he finished. Nodding toward the bathroom, he added, "Go on now, sugar, and get that shower, will you? Before I change my mind." *Or stand here like some idiot, fantasizing about joining you.*

Stress—that was all this was. Worry and grief, nothing more. Furious at his failure to maintain discipline, he swore beneath his breath, while Shannon wasted no time hurrying into the bathroom. The door clicked closed behind her, and he cursed again to hear it lock. But he couldn't say he blamed her, and besides that, he had more important worries at the moment.

Such as where the hell was Garrett? He should've checked in by now, at least. Though Rafe hated himself for it, he couldn't help but wonder if there had been any truth to Shannon's accusations.

Could a weak-chinned geek like Garrett really have had the balls to screw around on Lissa? Beautiful, sweet Lissa, who had finally turned around after her troubled teenage years and pulled her life together after meeting the straight arrow who would become her husband? But she was no fool, either. She would have known if something had been up with him, would have confided in the big brother who had raised her. And Rafe, when he'd returned from his deployment, would have torn the damned fool's head off, something he'd warned Garrett of when he'd flown in for the bachelor party. Though they had both been half-drunk that night, Rafe's warnings weren't the type that any sane man ever forgot. Especially a guy as "risk-averse," as Rafe's CO would have put it, as his brother-in-law had always been.

But as the shower hissed behind the closed door, Shannon's warnings about Garrett continued to prey on

Rafe's mind, making him wonder how much he really knew about his brother-in-law, who had always claimed he had no family, other than an estranged, alcoholic mother who had abused him for years. No friends, either, Lissa had once complained, other than the tech buddies he spent way too much time bonding with over some shoot-'em-up online game.

"He's so obsessed with his stupid 'Battle Bloodcraft,' I can't get him off the couch to paint the baby's room— or do a darned thing to help out when he finally drags home from work."

Rafe hadn't thought much about what had seemed like a minor domestic squabble, other than to grin at the idea that he and his fellow Rangers were living the adventure those geeks only dreamed of from their nice safe homes and mamas' basements. Yet now the word *obsessed* came back to make him wonder, and his anxiety only deepened when he repeatedly failed to reach Garrett on the prepaid cell phone he was using so law enforcement couldn't track them.

"This isn't right," Rafe grumbled before striding to the bathroom door. "Hurry up in there," he shouted, banging. "We may have to take off in a hurry."

But with Garrett driving the borrowed SUV, Rafe would need fresh wheels. Though he hated to compound his crimes, he reminded himself that during a combat mission, ordinary rules were made for breaking. Including the rules against grand theft auto, something he would have to resort to whether he decided to go in search of Garrett or relocate. Because one thing was for certain. He and Shannon couldn't stay here and take a chance on Garrett giving them away if he'd been picked up by either the local cops or their federal pursuers. And on the slim chance that Shannon's theory was right and

Garrett was somehow wrapped up in Lissa's murder, the consequences of his defection could be even deadlier.

SHANNON NEARLY JUMPED out of her skin when Rafe banged on the door and demanded she come out. She had barely finished rushing through her shower and hadn't yet toweled off, let alone had the chance to search the cramped space for anything she might use as a weapon should the opportunity arise. A shard from the mirror, a sharp sliver of chrome broken off the towel rack— she had learned from studying prisoner-made shanks and shivs that almost any item could be turned into a weapon, if one only had enough time.

"Let's go," Rafe called. "Unless you want this door coming down on your head."

She quickly dried herself, absurdly worried less about that threat than the idea that the huge Ranger would break in and find her naked. "Give me a minute. I'm just dressing. What's wrong?"

"Garrett," Rafe admitted. "He's still not back, and his cell phone's going straight to voice mail."

Reaching for her clothing, she couldn't resist smiling. "I thought you trusted him? Implicitly?"

"It's our luck I don't trust." Rafe's words were hard and empty as spent bullet casings. "Especially not with every law enforcement agent in this part of the country looking to bring us in."

She dressed in a rush, donning the same tan skirt she had been wearing since that morning, along with the T-shirt she had been given by the older woman. Finally slipping into her wedge-heeled sandals, she raked her fingers through her damp hair and spared herself one last look in the mirror.

She winced at what she saw. With neither makeup nor

a brush on her, and a purple lump high on her forehead, she looked like some sort of refugee—or like exactly what she was, the victim of an assault—by stun gun and abduction. No wonder Rafe hadn't jumped to take the bait when she'd trotted out whatever feminine wiles she could muster.

Thank God. She unlocked and opened the door to find him slinging his duffel over one broad shoulder.

He took one look at her and pulled a comb out of his pocket. "Here you go. Try this. Then we'll need to put the cuffs back on you."

Shaking her head, she said, "Forget the handcuffs. You won't need them. I've decided I'll be helping you. Helping find those babies."

"You're kidding, right?"

"It's the fastest way, maybe even the only way, to finish this before another family's shattered." Though she had only meant it as an excuse to convince him to leave her hands free, Shannon realized that what she was saying—what he'd tried to make her understand before—was true. Working in a small, targeted unit, with the support of hackers who couldn't care less about privacy laws, warrants or jurisdictions, they could cut weeks, or possibly months, from a cumbersome and complex official investigation.

They could prevent yet another expectant woman's murder.

All it would cost her was her honor, her career— and the betrayal of the oath she'd sworn to faithfully discharge the duties of her office. A vow she held as sacred as every hard-won lesson she'd gleaned from her father's storied career.

Even so, Rafe Lyons clearly didn't buy her supposed change of heart, because the moment she passed him back his comb, he snapped one of the cuffs onto her right wrist. After making an adjustment to the size, he snapped the other bracelet onto his own left hand— shackling them together before pocketing the key.

"It's not that I don't want to trust you." A smile quirked one corner of his mouth. "It's just that I'm no idiot. And there's way too much at stake to take any chances."

There was a rattle at the outer door, the scrape of a key before the door pushed open and was stopped by the security chain that kept it from going any farther than that first half inch. From the back of his waistband, Rafe produced a compact semiautomatic and aimed the handgun at the crack.

"It's me, Rafe. Let me in, will you? My hands're full, and—"

"Your head's empty?" Rafe demanded, dragging Shannon along as he moved to look through the crack before opening the door. "You had me worried, not answering your phone."

Garrett came in, several plastic shopping bags looped over his wrist and his hands filled with a pizza box that smelled of hot cheese, tomato and oregano. When Rafe had mentioned eating earlier, Shannon hadn't been interested in anything except finding some way to escape—or turn the tables on her captors. But now that her stomach had reawakened, it was howling urgent demands.

She was suddenly parched, too, and grateful that Garrett had thought of bringing sodas. Not exactly health food, but she found herself straining against Rafe's wrist in her eagerness to take the can Smith offered.

Turning her annoyance on Rafe, she argued, "Come

on, Lyons. Eating chained together is going to be a huge pain. For both of us."

Her stomach growled noisily, but Rafe ignored her as he stared a hole into Garrett and waited for his explanation. So the Ranger had been listening to what she'd told him after all. Maybe they would finally get some answers to the questions her investigation had raised.

Finally noticing Rafe's expression, Garrett stopped— the can of soda a frustrating two inches short of her hand. Paling visibly, he stammered, "When you called, I was busy paying for the pizza. I was fumbling for my wallet, worried about getting back, and—"

"So why not call me as soon as you got to the car? Unless you were tied up talking on the phone with someone else?"

"What're you saying?" Garrett slammed the can down beside the pizza box on the room's cheap laminate table, his voice turning defensive. "I've got a lot on my mind, that's all."

Shannon lowered her hand to stare a question at him. *Such as talking to your mistress?*

"I thought we agreed. Throwaway or not, if anyone figures out we're using these phones, our location can be pinned down. They're only for emergencies. Contacting each other. As I tried to contact you three separate times."

Garret's pallor gave way to an angry redness. "What is *with* you tonight?" Flinging a furious gesture in Shannon's direction, he accused, "She got to you while I was out picking up her damned things, didn't she? She's messing with your head, Rafe. Turning you against me."

Rafe's stare never wavered as he said, "Why don't

you set my mind at ease, then? Let me see that cell. I want to check your call log."

"I told you she'd be trouble. I warned you, Rafe. I did," Garrett shot back, making no move to hand over his phone.

As the silence lengthened, the weight of suspicion crushed the air from Shannon's lungs. Would Rafe, clearly in charge and all too handy with his weapons, continue to press a man he knew and sympathized with, or would the two of them unite against her?

Or was it possible that Rafe, still shackled to her, would decide Garrett was right about her and opt to leave her somewhere? A shallow grave sprang to mind, or maybe he would just leave her here in this room, dead.

She wanted to say something, to defend her earlier accusations. But instinct warned her that a single word could prove disastrous.

Rafe's hard gaze moved from Garrett to her, then back to the thin blond man.

With no warning at all, the tension exploded in a shattering burst. Before she could cry out or react at all, she was hurtled off her feet, landing hard on her back with Rafe thudding down across her.

With the breath knocked out of her, her rattled brain was slow to react, to piece together the continuing rain of shards behind the drawn curtains, now perforated with round holes.

Bullet holes, she realized as she spotted Garrett where he lay moaning on the floor, clutching at a burst of dark blood that had spread over the lower left sleeve of his white shirt. What she'd heard had been a spray of automatic gunfire coming through the window. What she'd felt was Rafe taking her down, his swift reflexes saving her life—maybe both their lives—in the process.

As he struggled to rise, Garrett clamped a hand over his forearm. "It hurts. God, it hurts. I've got to—"

"Stay down." Sliding off her but staying low, Rafe whispered to her, "Stay down, or I'll put you down for good—you understand that?"

Sinking back to the floor, Garrett stared around the room with wild eyes. From the parking lot outside, they heard a car alarm's shriek, but other than that, nothing. Neither voice nor siren made it past the eerie wail.

"Someone followed you, didn't they?" Rafe demanded. "You were so busy on your damned phone, you didn't even notice you had a cop on your tail."

"Not the police," Shannon whispered. "They wouldn't fire through that curtain blindly, especially not with me here."

"Good," Rafe said, digging the key from his jeans pocket and using it to unlock the cuff from his wrist. "Then we can return fire."

"Where'd you put my Glock?" she asked, as he crawled toward the duffel he'd been wearing over his shoulder moments earlier.

"You've got to be freaking kidding," he said through clenched teeth. "You just be a good girl and keep quiet—and stay out of my way."

With that, he unwrapped an AK-47 from his bag, which he dragged behind him as he crawled toward the window.

Riding a wave of pure adrenaline, she glared as fury flooded her veins. *Be a good girl and keep quiet?* As God alone knew who picked them off one by one?

While Rafe was distracted by an attempt to peer out the window without getting his head blown off, she scooted toward the duffel, reasoning that where he'd stowed one weapon, there could well be others.

What she meant to do with them, she had no idea, other than defending herself as best she could. *You could take out Lyons while his back is to you.* Garrett might not be armed—or in any condition to offer resistance.

Her heart stopped as a second burst of gunfire erupted, punching into the wall behind them. Instinctively, she dropped to her stomach, hugging the floor while creeping slowly forward. With her hand stretching before her, she drew close as Rafe thrust aside the ragged curtain's edge and returned fire.

The rattling boom was deafening and the swirling reek of gun smoke choking. Yet Shannon fought her way through it to grasp the duffel's strap and yank the bag in her direction, then reach inside. It was all she could do when she felt the butt of a familiar pistol under her hand.

"No!" Rafe bellowed, firing only once more before twisting clear of the window frame and turning his head away from the opening.

Startled by his shout, Shannon only gripped the pistol tighter.

Her next move was cut short by the sound of glass splintering against the window frame, followed by the whoosh of the flaming liquid that spattered over the remaining shreds of curtains. The cloth ignited instantly, falling inward as the thin fabric crumbled, feeding the fire with new fuel in the form of the nearby bedspread.

Shannon rolled away, coming up on her feet. Rafe was on her in an instant, his forward motion carrying her away from the open window toward the side of the motel room nearest the door. Garrett was there, too, his face a mask of terror as he cradled his useless right arm and yelled, "We have to get out of here!"

The room was blazing, the cheap, synthetic carpet filling the air with acrid smoke. Their attackers had pitched a Molotov cocktail, Shannon thought, though at this point the delivery system scarcely mattered. All that did—the only thing screaming through her brain—was the hideous decision they were faced with.

Stay there and burn to death in this motel room, or try to shoot their way free through the waiting ambush.

Chapter Five

"Into the bathroom." Rafe had to shout at Garrett to be heard over the earsplitting scream of the room's smoke detector. "I need you to fill the tub and wet some towels."

"We'll be trapped," Garrett protested, and Rafe saw raw panic in his white-rimmed eyes.

"Like hell," he said, turning the gun on his brother-in-law. "Now get in there right now, and don't come out until I tell you it's safe."

Garrett hesitated only a moment before nodding rapidly and doing as he'd been told.

Rafe closed the door, shutting the other man inside. "That'll keep him out of the way and busy for the moment." Probably on his knees and praying he would wake up on his own couch, where he could play the night away with his armchair adventures.

Shannon shifted her gaze from the spreading fire to him. "What's your plan?"

Rafe noticed she kept the sidearm she had recovered pointed in the direction of the window. He chose to interpret it to mean she had her priorities—namely, their immediate survival—in order for the moment. "We'll be going out the back door," he said.

She shook her head rapidly, the blue of her eyes

overlaid by the reflected dance of flame. "What back door? There's no back door here."

"There damn well will be in about five minutes," he insisted as picked up one of the oak chairs and hauled it toward the closet alcove along the back wall.

"Better make it two." She coughed on the smoke.

Looking over his shoulder, he nodded and prayed she wouldn't shoot him in the back the moment he turned away. "Keep covering the front, will you?"

With no choice except to trust her, he slung the assault rifle across his back and began slamming the chair legs against the wall. Fortunately this particular wall had at some point been remodeled using drywall, which crumbled before each punishing blow. But if the unit behind them, the one he meant to break into, still had its original plaster walls, then they could all be in huge trouble.

Even if he did break through, it was possible their attackers might be waiting on the other side. Or that another guest—an armed guest—might be staying in the room, although he would have to be stone-deaf or just plain stupid not to have fled the shooting and the shrieking smoke alarm already.

Chunk by chunk, the room's interior wall gave way, falling before his relentless onslaught as the sweat poured off his body. But as Rafe kept bashing, first one, then another, of the chair's legs snapped off.

"Hurry!" Shannon called.

The urgency in her voice had him turning his head to see yellow tendrils of flame licking up the far wall toward the ceiling. Ignoring the fire, he tossed aside the broken chair and lifted out the clothes rod. Positioning it like a lance, he took three steps backward and then slammed his body forward to finally punch through the stubborn wall.

More drywall gave way to his efforts, and he greedily sucked in the spill of sweet air. Kicking out one of the studs to widen the passage, he shouted back at Shannon, "Go get Garrett. Be quick."

The bark of gunfire was his only answer, and through the billowing smoke he spotted her—his captive federal agent—shooting through the window. Taking aim and firing as if she meant to kill.

WITH THE SWIRLING SMOKE making it nearly impossible to see into the darkness, Shannon squeezed off one last shot in the direction where she'd last spotted a man running, the black barrel of his automatic weapon jutting out in front.

Beyond that detail, she could make out nothing, not even the presence of a second man. But surely there were more. No sane shooter would try to take down an armed and desperate Ranger on his own. Unless Rafe had never been the target. Maybe he had been right. Maybe Garrett had picked up a tail in the form of some whacked-out thief with heavy firepower and a flair for guerrilla tactics.

No way. A garden-variety thief would never make this kind of assault rather than clipping Garrett when he'd headed for the door with his arms full of food and groceries. But what about a greedy family law attorney, desperate to keep his lucrative little empire safely hidden? Could Dominic Powers have somehow learned of Rafe's pursuit and hired a couple of local thugs or put up a reward to stop him from getting any closer?

Backing toward Rafe, Shannon bent low in an attempt

to stay below the level of the smoke. "That'll keep 'em under cover for a little bit."

As she reached the bathroom door, she opened it and ordered, "Come on, Garrett. Time to— Rafe, he's passed out. Going to need your help here."

Water was pouring into the nearly full tub, and Garrett lay beside it, slumped and bleeding on the worn linoleum floor. Before she could get to him, Rafe was pushing past her, shouting, "Go. Go on ahead. I've got him."

Shannon didn't waste a moment. Heart punching at her sternum, she rushed through the ash-filled heat to Rafe's ragged-edged "back door" and looked into a nearly pitch-dark room. An empty room, she prayed, as she pushed her way through the opening...

To freedom, which might or might not come with a bullet attached. But that was the chance she was duty-bound to take, and with ammunition still remaining in her gun—

She froze, remembering how her hand had brushed something else as she was reaching for her weapon. Money, she now realized—thick, banded packs of currency that reminded her how Rafe had emptied his accounts the day before his sister's funeral. His military credit union's teller had reported that he'd demanded all forty-eight thousand dollars in cash.

Without a moment's hesitation, Shannon squeezed back into the roiling smoke and grabbed the duffel. Pulling it through with her to the other side, she ignored the pang of guilt at the thought of separating a man from his hard-earned life's savings—savings he clearly meant to use to find and free his sister's missing child.

Shannon told herself she was wrong to focus on the merit of his crimes, wrong to consider anything but bringing him in as she'd been ordered. Or at least slow-ing him down enough so he could be recaptured without loss of life.

Stomach crowding into her throat, she crossed the room and reached the door leading outside, the door she could only pray remained unguarded. With her hand on the knob, she heard the sound of Rafe Lyons coughing—choking as he called out, "Help me. Help me—get him through."

If you run, he'll never catch you. You'll be home free. Safe. Steve, all your friends—everyone from work will be so relieved.

But running, leaving them to die, didn't feel like duty. It didn't taste of honor, either. Unable to bear the thought of leaving two men to burn to death in that in-ferno, Shannon turned back and helped Rafe maneuver the unconscious man through an opening that seemed determined to snag his clothes and trap both himself and his Ranger brother-in-law inside that smoke-filled oven.

Once they had Garrett through, Rafe was quick to follow, bending his knees to sling his brother-in-law over his shoulder. "Let's go," he ordered, his voice hoarse and his breaths ragged.

In the smoky dimness of a moment backlit by flame, Shannon looked into his eyes, and she saw something in them. Something that convinced her that this was a leader she had no choice but to follow, and that the best pathway out of hell was in a hero's wake.

Chapter Six

With at least one gunman out front and the wail of sirens drawing nearer, there was no way Rafe would risk all their lives by going around front to collect their borrowed Jeep. Instead he headed straight for the nearest vehicle, his sore lungs stinging and adrenaline roaring through his body.

With every muscle throbbing a mute protest, he set his brother-in-law back on his feet beside the older Accord, with its dark and peeling paint job.

"Garrett, wake up, buddy. Can you stand on your own a minute?"

Garrett murmured something and tried to open his eyes.

"I've got him." Shannon slipped beneath Garrett's uninjured arm to help support his weight and quietly reassured the injured man. "We'll get you somewhere safer. This is going to be all right."

"Thanks." Rafe pulled a folding multitool from his pocket, an item he'd found as handy as a fugitive as he had as a Ranger working on officially sanctioned missions. Tonight it proved indispensable in helping him jimmy the car's door lock and then pry off the cover to expose the steering column.

He tossed his rifle onto the passenger seat, and then

he was on his knees, leaning inside and working feverishly to strip the ignition wires. He heard Shannon pushing and hauling and goading Garrett into the backseat.
The moment he heard the rear door slam shut, Rafe's
heart sank with the certainty that she would take off
running while he had his hands full and his head below
the level of the dashboard.

He was going to lose her, despite the horrendous
risks he had taken to capture her and the critical role
she played in his plans to get inside Dominic Powers's
mansion—plans she would take back to both his military and civilian law enforcement pursuers. Still, there
wasn't one damned thing he could do to stop her. Even
if he could reach a weapon before she vanished into the
weedy brush beyond the parking lot, there was no way
in hell he was shooting down a federal agent. No way
he was hurting Shannon Brandt again.

*Forget her. Just keep your mind on surviving to
fight another day.* No sooner had the thought occurred
than the wires he was twisting sparked and the engine
coughed weakly—once, twice, a third time, before finally chugging to life on the fourth. As he scrambled
up into the seat, he heard a voice from outside.

"Heads down!" Shannon shouted an instant before
the thwack of bullets smacked the Honda like a lethal
hailstorm.

Slamming his door shut, Rafe reached for the gear-
shift as the sound of automatic gunfire—he recognized
the sound of his own AK—rattled from the spot where
Shannon stood, sheltered only by the dubious cover of
the car.

She was firing, he realized. Firing his weapon at their
enemy. While he was occupied, she must have grabbed

the assault rifle from the passenger seat and decided to use it to protect the three of them.

She swung inside, the muzzle of the AK-47 still smoking, and he took off, kicking up gravel with the rear tires. Leaving the headlights off, he squinted into the darkness, desperate to get the car around the rear of the motel and out onto the road.

And even more desperate to outrun their attackers and whatever authorities were even now responding to the gun battle and the fire.

"Turn. Turn right here!" Shannon shouted, an instant before he would have left the rutted parking lot and driven off into the weeds.

He wrenched the steering wheel, and the Honda's back end slewed around before the front tires caught and rocketed them forward, along the side of the building. Using the flashing lights of two fire trucks positioning themselves along the highway's shoulder as his guide, Rafe squeezed between the huge vehicles.

Ignoring the two firefighters shouting at him to stop, he rolled over the hose stretched between them, then put the pedal to the floorboard. The Honda rewarded him with more power than he'd expected, and he coughed and laughed at once, exhilarated by their close escape.

"You're having fun, are you?" Shannon sound furious. "Fun, while Garrett's back there bleeding, we all were very nearly killed, that motel's burning, and—and I—"

"I didn't pick this battle. Didn't want it, either. But we're all still breathing, aren't we? Don't I get to be happy about that?" He darted a look behind him, where Garrett was curled up and cradling his bleeding arm. "You're glad to be out of there, bro. Aren't you?"

Garrett groaned miserably in answer, clearly in no mood for celebration.

"I *shot* a man," Shannon finally finished, the fury pouring from her voice like water from a broken pitcher. In its wake, only despair remained. "I think I might have killed him."

"You've never killed before in the line of duty?" he asked as he scanned their mirrors for any sign of pursuit.

"I've killed." Her admission came on a trembling breath. "But never with intention."

The hollow ache in her words sent his mind flashing to those news items he had read. To the hostages in Iowa and the follow-up piece about the inquiry that had cleared her of wrongdoing, despite those who had gone to the media to question her judgment.

"It wasn't your fault. What happened back in—"

"I've never—never fired my weapon," she spoke over him, "except on the range and in training exercises."

"So now you have," he said flatly, his own first kill looming like a specter in his memory. The ghost of a militant insurgent who would have slain the men he'd been sworn to bring home safely. "Only you did it with *my* weapon, to save our lives from someone shooting at us."

"I didn't have to. Shouldn't have."

He had neither the time nor the energy to play shrink for her. "So what were you going to do, stand there and sing him a lullaby while he blasted away at us?"

"This isn't my fight."

"Last I noticed, those bullets and that Molotov cocktail were flying your way, too. Doesn't that make it your fight?"

"I had the chance to cut out before," she whispered,

not speaking to *him*, Rafe realized, so much as to herself. "To leave the two of you in that motel room."

Was she hearing in her mind the pronouncement of her next disciplinary review board? Or was she holding herself to an even higher standard—the impossible, imagined standard of a man killed when she was so young, he must be little more than legend to her?

"Well, thanks for being a human being about it," Rafe told her. "I would have hated to end up incinerated over your damned moral dilemma."

Seeing no pursuit, he turned on the Honda's headlights. As the dash lit up, he noticed that the fuel needle was only a hairsbreadth from the E. Great. Just what they needed, he thought, shoving the acquisition of another ride higher up on his priority list. Only next time he would take care to find a vehicle that would never be reported stolen.

Which meant, he realized, calling on another of his old friends. Relying on the bonds of military brotherhood to make even more of them accessories to his crimes.

He coughed again, his throat tightening against the lingering irritation from the smoke. For the first time he questioned whether he was doing the right thing, whether his plan could possibly succeed, and he felt a kinship, as unexpected as it was unwelcome, with the woman riding beside him, away from town and into darkness, and doubting herself and the choices she had made with every mile.

SHANNON COULD CALL IT SELF-DEFENSE, she knew. Could maybe even convince the higher-ups that she had acted out of fear for her own life as well as the lives of the two men she was committed to capturing alive, and that she'd stayed with them because she was waiting for a chance to turn the tables. But behind her back, her fellow special agents would always wonder. Was she so soft, so vulnerable, that she had given way to Stockholm Syndrome in a single day? Was that the reason she'd ignored a perfect opportunity to escape after she'd saved all their lives?

She had studied the phenomenon. In many ways it made sense that, over time, a helpless victim under threat of death would glom on to every "kindness" offered by her captor. A glass of water or a sandwich, a bandage for wounds he himself had inflicted—each "mercy" was a harbor in a raging sea of cruelty, a place of safety sheltering the psyche.

Over time the captive came not only to appreciate but to identify with her attacker. To abet the crimes against her, as so often happened when victims of abuse lied to protect their domestic partners. Sometimes it went further, and the victim was actually co-opted by her captors and sided with them, to the point of violence against her would-be rescuers. But *she,* Shannon told herself, was a trained field agent—a veteran who had spent five years patrolling the streets of Billings, Montana, and investigating crimes as a member of local law enforcement before joining the FBI.

She should know better. *Be* better. Should have shot the man firing on them and then raced into the weeds to hide when he had dropped. With sirens closing in and his brother-in-law bleeding in the backseat, Rafe wouldn't have risked coming after her, especially not if she'd kept hold of the assault rifle along with her own gun.

She knew that her choice to get into the car would later be analyzed and picked apart, dissected by her colleagues, most of whom were male and decidedly old-school in their thinking. Even if she managed to keep her badge, she was dead certain that in the future she would find herself relegated to desk duty—anywhere she wouldn't have to be trusted to make the right decision under pressure.

The career she had broken her tail working toward, the dream that had so long sustained her, was now over. Unless she somehow emerged from this a hero—the woman who, captive or not, brought down one of the cruelest criminal organizations in living memory. An organization that preyed upon the dreams of infertile couples, along the way slaking the avarice of its ring-leader with the blood of innocents.

Working from the inside, she would stop Dominic Powers and his people, would aid Rafe Lyons in his quest to find his stolen niece, as well as the locations of the other infants taken over the past year. And then she would bring in the Ranger—it was the only way.

She turned to watch him driving, the pink-yellow bars from the streetlights they passed slanting across his strong profile.

"I want you to know," she said tiredly, "I'm all in. I'm really going to help you. Of my own free will."

"Good to hear that—" Rafe slid a glance in her direction "—since I pretty much have my hands full and you're armed to the teeth."

She smiled, somehow infected by the wicked glint of humor in his eyes. Casting aside her lingering doubts, she felt an almost giddy relief—pride, even—to know that she had risen to the challenge of keeping them alive. The same feeling that must have whistled through him when he had laughed at their escape.

"Try to keep that in mind," she warned, as she raised

her right wrist, with its unwanted jewelry. "next time you think about cuffing me."

Reaching into his pocket, he dug out the key and passed it to her. "Here you go."

After unlocking the cuff, she rolled down the window and tossed the hated things onto the roadside.

"Hey, those are mine," Rafe protested. "And we might need them later to—"

"Save it," she said, all too aware that he was likely to have at least one other set. And that he could all too easily incapacitate her with or without hardware, should he choose to.

Ignoring the displeasure radiating from him, she turned in her seat to check on Garrett, who was lying in a semi-fetal position behind Rafe. "How's the arm, Garrett? Has the bleeding slowed up any?"

To her eye, it looked like it had, but she didn't get an answer. She reached back to shake his leg, and he blinked at her, his face a mask of pain. "I need a hospital," he burst out. "Demerol or morphine—some kind of painkiller."

"Sorry, man," Rafe told him. "But hospitals and physicians are required to report all gunshot wounds."

"So drop me off," he pleaded. "I don't care. It feels like somebody's snapped my arm in two. Like it could fall off any minute."

"I know this is hard. Know firsthand it hurts like hell to be shot," Rafe said. "But you've got to hang in there with us. Your daughter's counting on you."

"I thought I could do it, but I'm not cut out for this. Not like you. You don't need me to find her. Just kick down those doors, the two of you. Wave your guns in the guy's face 'til he tells you where she is."

"We both know it won't be that easy. And without

your hacker connections, we might never pin down the locations of those—"

"I don't care about that," Garrett wailed.

"Don't you care about Amber Lee?" Shannon demanded, suddenly impatient with the man's whining. The pain and fear she understood, but bailing on his daughter was unforgivable. "And what about your wife? Don't you care what they did to Lissa? And Rafe? He's giving up *everything* to go after Powers. You don't think you owe it to them to—"

"Of course I care, but I can't do this. I'm bleeding and I'm weak, and I'm slowing you two down."

"You are damned well going to man up, right this minute." A snarl contorting his face, Rafe spoke in a voice that filled the car. "Make the choice to pull yourself together and I *will* get you through this. But give me reason to believe you don't *want* this mission to go forward and—"

"We'll find a drugstore," Shannon suggested, thinking that whether he was innocent or guilty, the hope of relief might be more effective than a death threat. "Pick up some supplies and painkillers, and get you all fixed up."

Beside her, she heard Rafe huff out an exasperated sigh before he followed her lead. "And we'll find someplace to rest and eat," he promised. "You'll feel better in the morning. And then you'll remember what's at stake here. What's worth more than any of our lives."

Chapter Seven

Madison Rothschild Worth couldn't believe she had allowed her husband to talk her into thinking that a baby—a bitty girl to cuddle, dress in cute designer outfits and show off to her friends—would finally ease her grief. But every time she held it—or *her,* as the much older, wiser Everett was always reminding her she should say—all she could think of was stroking Suki's soft fur and dressing the tiny white Maltese in the extensive wardrobe she had purchased in the Beverly Hills doggie boutiques that she still loved to frequent.

Tears followed, the same sobs that wracked her body every time she thought of her last glimpse of her angel, limp and broken, in the jaws of the filthy coyote that had come up from the canyon to raid their hillside backyard—the one place Maddi had always felt it was safe to let her precious three-pound teacup darling play and sniff, though always under her own watchful supervision.

She reminded herself, as her husband had reminded her whenever he wasn't off somewhere filming on location, that it had been more than two years now, that her other friends had by now all given up their tiny hairballs and moved on to coddling babies, as she should do, though the doctors said her years-long struggle with anorexia ruled out a pregnancy of her own. But he didn't understand. This squirming, fussy, soggy-diapered creature he had brought home was not and would never be her child.

Poor lost Suki was her baby. Her only darling girl, and no other puppy—not even this human mongrel, who had come from heaven only knew what sort of bloodlines—would ever do.

Lip curling in disgust, Maddi used the intercom to call the nanny. "Come and take it, please, Consuelo. Mommy's got another of her headaches—and this diaper's stinking the place up to high heavens, besides."

RAFE WAS STILL KEYED UP two hours later as he was meeting with a friend of a former associate—a grim-faced man with a cleft chin and short hair prematurely silvered at the temples—in the empty parking lot of a closed grocery store to exchange the Honda for a fairly new black Yukon. As they traded vehicles, neither asked the other questions, though Rafe did notice the quick scan the newcomer gave Shannon.

Rafe held his breath, his muscles tensing and his mouth drying in an instant. Though the lot was dark and the inland town he'd chosen tiny, would she make some outcry anyway despite what she told him earlier? Plead with his contact to take a message to her superiors or family, perhaps some boyfriend who would be anxiously awaiting her return?

For some reason the thought of a potential lover bothered Rafe more than he knew it should. Probably because if some SOB ever stole a woman like this one from him, he knew he would waste no time hunting down the kidnapper to reclaim her. And, as likely as not, killing the bastard in the process.

Shannon studied the stranger, too, but whether it was the buzzed, military-style haircut or the look in the man's eye, she quickly turned away to help Garrett into the SUV's rear seat.

"Brought some clothes, first aid kit—a few other things I thought you might need," the stranger told Rafe before handing him a set of keys. "You'll find a map to the cabin on the front seat. Just an old family place on a backwater slough—buddy of mine rehabbed it as a fish camp getaway. Nothing fancy, but it has all the basics."

Rafe shook the man's hand and said, "Thanks. I—I don't know what to say."

"Sua Sponte." The Rangers' Latin motto, meaning *Of their own accord.*

Rafe's throat tightened in comprehension, in the knowledge that as alone as he had felt since first learning of his sister's murder, there were men he knew—even some he didn't—who supported his unsanctioned mission. Men moved by brotherhood and conscience, who were willing to risk careers or military pensions, possibly their freedom, to help him in his quest. Of their own accord.

All because they knew he was a Ranger, a Ranger whom trusted fellow Rangers had told them was doing right.

While Rafe headed back north toward Lake Okeechobee, Shannon sat in the backseat with Garrett.

"Don't try to take the shirt off yet," she urged quietly. "That'll only start it bleeding again. Just wrap your arm up in this towel for right now, and let me see what's in the kit—look at this. You're in luck."

Rafe heard the rattle of what sounded like pills in a bottle.

"What is it?" Garrett's voice sounded thin, exhausted. "You know what? I don't even care. Just give 'em to me. Please."

"Hold on," Shannon told him. "There's a label. That's some friend you've got, Rafe. Antibiotics, and some oxycodone for pain."

Garrett whimpered, "Thank God. Let me have three of them."

"You'll get one," she said. "With the antibiotic."

Garrett complained, even went so far as to appeal to Rafe to intervene, but in the end he sipped from one of the fast-food sodas they had picked up from a drive-through window, along with the burgers the injured man had refused. Within twenty minutes he had settled and very soon dropped off to sleep.

"Thanks for that," Rafe told her as he turned onto a thin thread of a gravel road, exactly one-point-eight miles from the bait shop, as the directions had indicated. The tires crackled over pebbles, and the Yukon wallowed over washed-out ruts at a much-reduced speed.

"Poor Garrett," Shannon murmured. "He's going to hate it when we finally have to clean up that wound."

"So you're feeling sorry for him now?" Rafe challenged. "Weren't you the one suggesting before that he had something to do with Lissa's murder? Or was that only for my benefit—your divide and conquer strategy?"

"It wasn't a ploy. I was telling you what I know," she insisted. "There definitely was—probably still is—a girlfriend, and Garrett could have known about the neighbor."

"Could have? You seemed positive before."

"The neighbor was convincing. But sometimes people on the periphery have their own motives for the stories they report. A personal grudge, a need to gain attention—for all we know the man could have been having an affair with—"

"Not with Lissa. She would never," Rafe insisted.

"I didn't mean to imply—"

"She was bent on turning into a bona fide earth mother," Rafe said, remembering, his stomach churning with the greasy burger he'd consumed. "Sewing little organic cotton dresses, collecting recipes for homemade baby food—all natural. She would've been... Would've made the most amazing mom. I can almost see her. Hear her, singing to her little girl..."

Unable to go on, Rafe cursed the smoke from the motel for his stinging eyes and choking hoarseness.

He felt a warm weight, the caress of Shannon's hand against the side of his neck. An offer of compassion from a woman he had kidnapped, a woman he had nearly gotten killed this very night.

"I have a brother," she confided. "We don't always get along so well, but if anybody ever went after him..."

Though she left the rest unspoken, he thanked God she was at least pretending to understand what he was feeling. What he was doing, out of desperation and the fear that the authorities were hamstrung by the rules. Remembering her kindness toward Garrett, a man she suspected could be involved in the ugliest of crimes, he wondered if empathy might be a deep-seated part of who she was. A facet of her personality too strong to suppress no matter what the situation.

We'll see how sweet she acts if she takes you into custody. He let himself imagine her pistol at his back, her smug description of her victory once she was in earshot of her fellow agents, their laughter over how skillfully she'd played him to make the bigger bust. The moment she was finished, she would turn him over to the Army and see him locked in Leavenworth so fast, his head would spin.

He would do well to remember that, for him, that was one of only two places this journey could end. The other, an unmarked grave, seemed far more likely....

It didn't matter. He'd already made peace with the high price of his final duty to his little sister. From the day he had failed to report for duty, punched out the joke of a burned-out police detective assigned to Lissa's case, then taken off with his own money and weapons, the die had been cast, and with his abduction of a special agent, the stakes had only risen.

Garrett had been dead set against it, but his discovery that the woman baiting them with "information" was an FBI operative had come at nearly the same time Rafe had connected with a real source, a woman who worked in Powers's household, who had assured him that no one except a woman—an "invisible" domestic— had a prayer of getting inside. And not just any woman would do. They needed someone who could keep her head under pressure. Someone exactly like the clever and clearheaded special agent who'd been working to entrap him.

Still, Rafe realized, though risking his own life had become almost second nature to him, risking those of civilians was another matter altogether. Garrett's injury drove home the possibility that he, too, could be killed, orphaning the child they were fighting to bring home. Shannon, too, could fall victim to this fool's quest—a sacrifice that had been far easier to justify before he'd met her.

"The neighbor has a wife, too," Shannon admitted. "And she has a social network habit. She posted about the vacation on her Facebook page and was pretty loose with details about how long they'd be away."

Irritation needled at him because she hadn't told him sooner, followed by reluctant admiration for the way she'd played the cards she held. Before he could comment, however, a pair of dark shapes materialized before the headlights, and he had to jam on the brakes to avoid a pair of whitetails out for an unhurried night-time browse. As the SUV jerked to a halt, Shannon gasped and Garrett started, waking with a sharp grunt of pain.

"Sorry about that," Rafe told them, before turning to address a couple of the most laid-back deer he'd ever seen. "Move it, you two, or I promise you, we'll be having venison for dinner."

The deer strolled back into the thick trees, and he rolled forward until the Yukon's high beams lit the ex-terior of a cypress cabin, weathered and homely and raised off the ground on blocks.

"We ought to be fine, unless it rains," he said, study-ing the low-hanging porch roof, which was missing more than a few shingles.

As they climbed out of the car, Shannon eyed the structure dubiously. "Or someone strikes a match. If you don't mind, cowboy, I've about had my fill of fires for one evening."

"You and me both, Shanno—Special Agent." He turned to grab his duffel, his sense of alarm sending up flares at how close he'd come to calling her by name. Thinking of her more as a person than a resource to be used, collateral damage in a mission in which she had no stake.

He would do well to keep her role in mind, to keep himself at arm's length. Otherwise he would never be able to do what he had sworn to do, to risk a sacrifice that might well stand between him and the innocent child he would stop at nothing to save.

Just remember, Shannon Brandt's nothing more than another means to the most important end of your life. Not a civilian or a fellow Ranger—and especially not a gorgeous woman you can ever think of claiming as your own.

Chapter Eight

Unincorporated Okeechobee County
August 23, 6:48 p.m.

"This is crazy," Shannon insisted two nights later. Sitting at the rough bench across from Rafe, she rubbed at the small of her back, which was beaded with perspiration in this un-air-conditioned sweatbox.

Her body was already dreading the thought of another night spent tossing and turning on one of the cabin's Spartan bunks. And mentally, she was no better off, stressed over what her family, friends and coworkers must be thinking and fed up with all the waiting and the plotting, the hours she'd spent cooped up watching over Garrett while Rafe gathered the things they would need for their mission.

And then there was the mission itself, an insane gamble that seemed all too likely to get one of them killed. Maybe not Garrett, since he would be staying behind with his newly purchased laptop, tethered to the internet via the smartphone provided by another of Rafe's contacts.

Hair stirring with the breeze of the ancient oscillating fan they had set up on the small table, Shannon slid a look in Garrett's direction, wondering for the hundredth time if the computer security specialist had what it took to control his fear and pain, and handle his part of the plan. Certainly he looked better since Rafe had sterilized his wound and removed what had turned out to be not a bullet but a teardrop-shaped shard of glass embedded deep inside his elbow.

Or at least Rafe thought he was better, and considering how handy the Ranger had been with those tweezers and the sterile dressings, she was inclined to believe he had plenty of experience patching up his fellow soldiers in situations where no medics were available.

Garrett looked up from his laptop, where he had been clumsily plunking his way through keystrokes one-handed. His foot was twitching, tapping, as Shannon had noticed that it often did when he was stressed. "Think I could take another pain pill?"

"That computer have a clock, bro?" Rafe snapped, his eyes turning hard.

He might have had more tolerance, thought Shannon, if Garrett's phone hadn't been lost the night of the motel fire. Since then, they had argued about it several times, with Rafe insisting—for her benefit, she was certain—that he was only worried about what a pursuer might glean if the phone had been recovered. But Shannon knew, they all knew, that he was angry he had never had the chance to check his brother-in-law's call log.

"If you're done over there, you should come and eat," Shannon suggested. Thin to start with, Garrett had been living on Diet Cokes and those pain pills, which she suspected he was using as an emotional escape. But as irritating as he'd been in the past few days, they needed his skills and contacts to have a chance of success.

Which meant she had to do all she could to make sure he kept himself in operating order—even if it meant playing peacemaker between Rafe, who was keeping the pain pills in his pocket, and the man she was frightened to think she would be forced to rely on.

Stringy-haired and sweating, Garrett stood up from his bunk to join them, his laptop left open. Rather than sitting beside Rafe, he chose a spot across the table, though it forced him to share a bench with Shannon.

"Here you go," she said, unwrapping half a Cuban sandwich for him, a savory mix of roast pork, ham, Swiss cheese and pickle on a roll flattened between hot metal plates.

In response to her pleas for dietary mercy after two days of canned and fast food, Rafe had picked up a colorful salad with grilled chicken and sliced fruit for her. She speared a juicy yellow chunk of mango and pointed it at the Ranger. "What if this Mrs. Rodriguez decides to sell you out to Powers instead of claiming I'm her niece?"

"Not gonna happen, sugar," Rafe said, his cockiness annoying her even more than the West Texas accent and patronizing pet name. "Considering how much I paid her and what a bullying jerk Powers is with his help, she pretty much jumped at the opportunity."

Noting the way he had oversold his plan, she took the "pretty much" part as a warning. The overworked owner of a small-time cleaning service, Paloma Rodriguez must have reservations—and she'd had days to think about what a man as vile as Dominic Powers would do to any woman who betrayed him.

"We'd better hope he treats the help—namely me— better than his former wives." She shook her head at the thought of the missing first spouse, who was no doubt in a landfill somewhere or at the bottom of the ocean. "Or this is going to be one short mission."

"His bodyguards are always the ones who search the women. They'll pat you down for weapons, a cell phone and probably cheap thrills as you come off the Rodriguez Cleaning van."

"Lovely. Thanks for giving me a goon-groping to look forward to."

"Sorry." Rafe looked unhappy but resigned to this part. "But it's better you prepare yourself, so you won't haul off and do something that draws way too much attention."

"Like putting some perv in a chokehold until he cries for his mama?"

Rafe grinned and snorted. "Exactly like that, much as it would turn me on to see it."

When she rolled her eyes, he quickly got back to business. "Once you get inside, the best thing you can do is stay as far from Powers as possible. Guy's paranoid as hell, so it's better if he doesn't get a good look at you or hear your voice."

"I'm not sure why that would be a problem." Using the laptop connection, they had been stunned to find no mention of her abduction, an Army Ranger's disappearance or the murder that had set the whole incident in motion. Which meant the authorities were tightly controlling the flow of information. Did her bureau superiors imagine they were protecting her somehow—or was it the military, not wanting to alarm the public with the news that a decorated hero had gone rogue? It was also possible they already suspected Shannon had willingly gone with him, that somewhere in the course of their previous communications she had fallen for Rafe Lyons. Whichever was the case, Shannon counted it as an advantage that neither Powers nor his men were likely to recognize her.

Rafe shook his head. "Trouble is, Mrs. Rodriguez is about four-eleven, with curly black hair and a dark complexion. She came from Cuba thirty years back, but it might as well've been last week, if you listen to her accent."

Shannon shrugged. "So I'm from the taller American side of the family."

"Maybe a little too American for him to buy you as part of Rodriguez Cleaning. Especially with those blue eyes. But don't worry. I've got that part all taken care of."

"What do you mean?" she asked.

Before Rafe could respond, Garrett put down his half-eaten sandwich and announced, "It's time, I think. Time to take that pain pill."

Rafe gave an exasperated snort. "You'd think you got nailed by heavy artillery and not a tiny piece of glass."

"A huge shard. And your digging around in there didn't help at all," Garrett grumbled. "Probably got it infected."

"Go get a shower, if you're so worried about germs."

"There's no hot water, and that shower stall looks like it hasn't been scrubbed in decades."

"I cleaned it myself, and anyway, you're starting to smell like you haven't been scrubbed in decades, either. Now go. You'll feel better. Then I'll give you that pill."

Cursing under his breath, Garrett shoved the remains of his dinner back inside the bag before heading straight to the cabin's tiny bathroom. Less than a minute later they heard the groan of rusty pipes.

Shannon gave Rafe a look and swallowed her last bite

of chicken. "Do you really trust him in this condition? Listen to him. He's been acting like a—"

Scowling, he shook his head. "He's normally not a bad guy. But who wouldn't flake out after finding his wife the way he did and the stress of these past few weeks on the run? This is not a man who's used to having firebombs and bullets coming his way."

"Let me point out one thing." She stood up from the bench and started toward the bottom bunk Garrett had claimed. "Tomorrow morning you expect me to climb into that van with strangers, any one of whom could decide to sell me out, and head into a butcher's house without weapons or a backup—all while trusting Garrett Smith with my life."

"I'll be watching him," Rafe assured her. "Trust me on this, Shannon."

She stopped halfway across the room and looked back toward Rafe. Realizing for the first time that he hadn't called her Brandt or Agent or even the condescending "sugar." This time he had called her by her given name.

"You're too important to me—to my mission—for me to leave anything to chance."

Tossing up her hands, she said, "This is all chance. Don't you see that? The chance that a nearly thirty-year-old, clearly Anglo woman—who barely remembers a handful of words from Spanish One in high school—won't stick out like a sore thumb. The chance I'll have the time alone to sabotage the security system... The chance they'll call you in for the repairs, instead of having someone they know on retainer. And worst of all, the chance that Garrett hasn't sold us out."

Rafe jumped out of his seat and in two strides he was right there, towering over her. "Why would he? Can you explain that? Even if he'd really wanted Lissa dead, what could Garrett possibly have to do with Powers? It's beyond belief. Ridiculous. He wanted to come with me, begged to help me find his missing child and take out his wife's killers."

Shannon didn't take a step back. Didn't give a single inch but instead studied the tiny spokes of golden brown on the field of green in his eyes, the shadow of dark beard that vied with the specter of grief and worry. And the fierce loyalty that, in this case, might prove to be his fatal flaw.

"I'm checking out that laptop," she said, gesturing to the computer Garrett had left open. And hoping that, in his rush to get cleaned up so Rafe would give him another pain pill, Garrett might have forgotten to cover his tracks just this once.

Rafe's lips, those lips she tended to notice all too often, pressed into a hard line, and disapproval etched two grooves into his forehead. But rather than forbidding her, he nodded, said unhappily, "You've earned that right by this time. But you won't find anything."

With that, he headed for the door to the wide front porch where he had spent much of the past two days. Simply staring, or at least that was how it would have appeared to anyone who didn't see beneath the surface. But Shannon had long since realized there was far more to the man than he'd allowed her to see. Far more swirling in the depths behind those moss-green eyes.

More despair, more pain, more vulnerability than he was willing to show anyone. Did the men he led, including Garrett, even see it? Or did they only know the competent leader, the consummate warrior whose persona he wore like a suit of armor?

An urge blindsided her, the desire to forget what she'd

said about Garrett and go to Rafe instead. Dismissing it immediately, she went to the computer, her mind reciting the symptoms of Stockholm Syndrome like a surgeon general's warning.

Handsome, troubled, even as admirable as she found Rafe, she had grown up a horse-obsessed tomboy on a Western ranch—a far cry from the kind of woman to be derailed from something of this much importance by a virile male body that called to hers. Irritated with herself, she reined in her thoughts and got down to the task at hand.

Knowing Garrett would be in a huge hurry to finish his shower, she put a finger to the touchpad. The black screen flared to life but revealed nothing more interesting than a popular search engine with the words Palm Beach in the find box. Disappointed, she moved quickly, checking the search history.

It was nothing but a blank, a sign that Garrett had been sharp enough to wipe any record of the places he had visited online. Given that he worked in cyber security, she wasn't surprised he'd made erasure a habit— either that or he'd installed some sort of subroutine to keep the information from being recorded in the first place.

Her frustration peaked when she heard the high squeal of the shower being shut off. But with no other windows open and no sign of programs running...

Wait, she thought, then pressed the CTRL-ALT-DELETE keys simultaneously to bring up the task manager and check for other processes running in the background. She found a list, but for the most part wasn't sure what she was seeing—except for one. Could that possibly be...?

A few keystrokes later she had it up, the online role-playing game known as "Battle Bloodcraft." Though she had never played, she knew that the addictive nature of the game had come under fire, with reports of students dropping out of school, people losing their jobs and marriages destroyed because of endless hours spent playing.

Was this what Garrett had been doing last night? Playing games while he was supposed to have been working on the viral payload she would introduce to gain access to Powers's computer?

Before she could call Rafe in to see what she'd found, a small textbox popped up in the lower right corner of the screen.

ANGELEYES81: where u been??? need u bad now! please!

Shannon glared in the direction of the bathroom. If Garrett came out right now, she might throttle him personally. It was bad enough that he would be gaming online with anyone, putting them all at risk. It hadn't taken a genius to figure out that ANGELEYES81 was the mysterious and decidedly unsaintly girlfriend. They had tried serving a subpoena to the "Battle Bloodcraft" people to learn the woman's true identity, but the megarich company—run by the game's obnoxious twenty-four-year-old creator—had a legal dream team fighting this "breach of customer privacy" in federal court.

Deciding on the spot to find out all she could, Shannon sneaked a quick peek at the still-closed bathroom door. Hearing nothing from inside, she clicked the reply tab and quickly typed the first response that popped into her mind. Anything to try to get the conversation going.

GARR_GOYLE69: Please what?

ANGELEYES81: let me meet u! have to c u again, explain! where r u right now?

There it was, thought Shannon. An onscreen confirmation there was a relationship.

But something made her hesitate to call the Ranger. Made her press for more before the opportunity was over.

GARR_GOYLE69: Too risky! Wouldn't be right being together right now after my wife and baby...you know.

And then she waited. And waited, her fingers shaking and dread pooling in her stomach. Dread of learning that Garrett Smith had been involved in what had happened to his family.

Though she couldn't imagine him personally killing Lissa, if he'd been somehow complicit, she couldn't imagine how she could explain that to Rafe, then manage to prevent him from killing Garrett on the spot, no matter what it cost him.

A footstep was her only warning before Garrett, just behind her, bleated out a panicked, "Get away from there!"

But it was too late already, for even as Shannon leaped to her feet, one final message popped up in the corner of the screen.

A message that made all the difference in the world.

Chapter Nine

The night music of ten thousand frogs and tiny insects gave way to shouting—shouting Rafe easily heard through the screened window. Rushing inside from the porch, he spotted the normally nonconfrontational Garrett crowding Shannon, who was trapped by the close confines of the lower bunk where she was sitting.

His face red and his eyes wild, Garrett was raging like a madman, screaming that she had no business invading his privacy and risking their only computer.

"You're the one putting every one of us at risk downloading your stupid game and logging on to—"

"Since when do you run my life?" Garrett yelled into her face.

Though Rafe had every confidence she could kick his brother-in-law's legs from under him and step on his scrawny neck before he knew what hit him, raw instinct made him cross the room and seize his brother-in-law to yank him back from her.

Without meaning to, Rafe grabbed Garrett's injured arm, eliciting an agonized yelp. Color draining from his face, Garrett went limp, and Rafe had to support him to keep him from collapsing.

"Sorry I had to hurt you," Rafe said, oddly relieved at this evidence that Garrett hadn't been faking his discomfort to score the pain pills for other reasons. "But you need to shut up and tell me what's going on here."

Glaring at Garrett, Shannon pointed at the screen. "I don't know why he's so upset," she said in a voice dripping with sarcasm. "I was only chatting with his girlfriend."

Rafe's jaw clamped tight, shoving Garrett away as if he were radioactive, his hands tightening into a pair of rock-hard fists.

Garrett swayed on his feet for a moment before sucking in a panicked breath, his gray eyes darting from Rafe to Shannon, then back at the greater threat.

"So she was right?" Rafe demanded, his barely controlled fury a rushing noise in his ears. "The agent here was right when she told me you were cheating? Screwing around on my little sister, who was so excited about having your baby?"

Garrett shook his head rapidly. "No—I would never, never cheat on Lissa. You've got it all wrong!"

"Then enlighten us," Shannon ordered.

"It's just—it's just I was so stressed out. The pressures of my job, the extra work I was taking on the side to help make ends meet, since Lissa wasn't working. And then there was Lissa, obsessing over every little detail about the baby…."

Teeth clenching until they ached, Rafe said, "Don't you dare make this about her. Blame my little sister for your—"

"I don't." Now Garrett's tears were spilling, his face blotching with emotion. "It was all me, just trying to escape for a while, blow off a little steam."

"In hotel rooms you were renting while you were supposed to be at work?" asked Shannon, driving yet another nail into the coffin of Rafe's faith in his brother-in-law.

"Let me finish, please." Garrett's damp eyes were pleading as he looked from one of them to the other. "Please, Rafe, don't look at me like that."

"Like what? You mean like a lying, cheating dirt-bag?"

"You've got to hear me out," Garrett begged.

Folding his arms across his chest, Rafe turned his back. Because if he had to look at Garrett one more second, he was afraid he was going to knock his brother-in-law's teeth down his throat.

"The guys I contract to field-test my systems," Garrett blurted, "they were always going on about this game they were into. It sounded pretty awesome, a great way to burn off steam, you know? So I could be a better husband."

"Let me get this straight," Rafe said. "You were taking marital advice from a bunch of outlaw hackers."

"Not marital advice—of course not. It just sounded… It really is a cool game—a place where I could… This game—it's like another world. A world where I'm not just a low-level computer nerd, I'm some kind of…" He gave a helpless shrug, his face a mask of misery. "A hero—that's the real joke, isn't it? A guy like me, wanting to feel like a big man—like you—and ending up betraying the one w-w-woman who loved me just the way I was."

"Tell us about this Angeleyes," Shannon said. "Is that how you met her?"

"No, no. I'm trying to tell you, you've got that wrong. Angel's one of my testers, that's all. I've worked with him for years."

Rafe whipped around. "With him? You mean you were meeting some guy for sex in those hotel rooms?"

Garrett laughed.

"You find this funny?"

Sobering abruptly at the threat in Rafe's expression, Garrett said, "No, sorry. I was only thinking what Angel'd have to say about the idea of him and me... He likes to think of himself as a kind of hacker Lothario, a real ladies' man."

"So are you trying to say," Shannon put in, "that you weren't meeting this man, this Angel, physically but online during these assignations you set up?" No wonder she hadn't been able to get an ID on the woman.

"They weren't assignations, they were battles. In the game world, you know? Crucial battles...or at least that's how I saw them at the time."

"So let me get this straight," said Shannon. "You were ditching work—"

"And Lissa," Rafe interrupted.

"And your pregnant wife," Shannon continued, "to sneak off to play this game where no one would interrupt you? And these text messages we subpoenaed weren't to some illicit lover but a hacker buddy you teamed up with to play out your little hero fantasy?"

Garrett's face went crimson. "I'm an idiot. I know that."

"You're a junkie," Rafe accused. "Addicted to that cyber-crack when you had a great life, the kind of real life a lot of guys would fight and die for. High-tech, well-paying job, beautiful young wife who adored you, first kid coming."

"Don't you think I know that now?" Garrett exploded, his reddened eyes streaming tears. "Don't you think it's been killing me, knowing how much time I wasted?

How I wasn't there for Lissa, wasn't home protecting her and our baby, all because of some stupid game?"

"Yet you're still playing, aren't you?" Rafe challenged. "Downloading the game to this computer, so your hacker pal can find out where we are. What else did you tell him? That I was paying for everything in cash and had plenty of it? Did you email him a road map to that motel?"

Garrett's head shook so rapidly, it looked as if it might fly off at any moment. "No, I didn't. Of course I didn't. Yeah, I played the game a little, just to de-stress when I couldn't sleep nights. But this is my child, Rafe—my baby girl—we're out searching for. Do you honestly believe I'd risk her life and ours by doing anything so stupid?"

Rafe shook his head, his grief a leaden weight sinking through his chest. "I don't know what I honestly believe about you right now."

"Believe this," Garrett vowed to him. "I'm done with 'Battle Bloodcraft,' permanently retired, and I'm finished texting Angel, or any of the guys, about the game. Any time you want, you can check my phone, the laptop. The only time I'll talk to them is when we need their help."

Rafe thought about that for a moment before saying, "One question," and turning to look at Shannon. "I know you thought it was a woman, but were you right about the rest? Did he have anything to do with Lissa's death? Anything at all?"

"No!" Garrett shouted, a shriek of either agony or mortal terror.

An extremely well-founded terror, thought Rafe, who imagined leaving his brother-in-law in tiny pieces along this isolated inlet—bloody bits to feed the local alligator population—if he'd been somehow involved in Lissa's death in any way.

"I would never, ever hurt her," Garrett persisted. "I might've been a little freaked out, but I loved her, loved that baby from the second I found out I was going to be a father."

Shannon met his eyes. "All the victims we've found have been connected to an online survey, a survey they took from a baby gift registry promising a free stroller for fifteen minutes of their time. Did you know about it, Garrett? Did you hear about those other women's murders before Lissa's?"

"No!" Garrett cried. "How can you think—"

Rafe stepped in then. "So now you think Garrett was some sort of copycat using those killings as a cover to get rid of his own wife and baby? I'm willing to bet you didn't turn up a single bit of evidence to back it up."

"No," she admitted. "That's why I'm asking him right now, point blank."

"And I'm telling you, I had no idea about the web survey or the other women until my friends from the hacking community tracked down the information after…after Lissa was…" Garrett's voice trailed off.

"Apparently, this 'Angeleyes' doesn't think he's guilty, either," said Shannon. "Come and have a look at this, keeping in mind it was me typing Garrett's side of the conversation."

Pushing past Garrett, Rafe scanned the chat messages Shannon pointed out, right down to the final line.

ANGELEYES81: who cares what it looks like? U had nothing 2 do with what happened to her.

"Is this true?" Rafe studied Garrett's face intently. "Swear it to me, bro. Swear you had nothing to do with it, and pray I never find a shred of evidence you're lying, or I swear you'll never see that little girl of yours."

Garrett straightened, his expression sober, and wiped his arm across his damp face before summoning the courage to look Rafe directly in the eye. "You won't. Because I would never in a thousand years even have thought up something like—like that hell I walked into. Please, Rafe. Sure, I screwed up, betrayed your sister by not being there when I should have been. It was my fault, completely my fault, but I—"

Shannon touched his hand and in a gentler voice said, "They only would have killed you, too, if you had been home. It happened in a couple of the other cases."

Shaking off her touch as if it repelled him, Garrett kept his gaze locked onto Rafe's. "If you want to hurt me for failing to protect her, I know I have it coming. If you want to slug me 'cause of my—my problem with the game, I accept that, too."

Rafe thought about that, but the sincerity in Garrett's face, the obvious remorse, stayed his hand.

Garrett took it as permission to finish speaking his piece. "Whatever I've done, I can promise you, it will haunt me for the rest of my life. A life I intend to spend making it up to Lissa's memory by being the best—the very best—father I can for our daughter."

"All I ask is that you mean every word of that." Rafe's voice shook as he leaned in, his eyes only inches from Garrett's. "Every syllable."

"So help me God," Garrett vowed, raising his right hand like a Boy Scout.

Rafe nodded, swallowing a red-hot coal of anger. Willing to do this much—to do whatever it took— only for the sake of a tiny infant he might never live to meet.

August 25, 6:34 a.m.

SHE LOOKED LIKE a completely different person. Staring into the mirror of the budget hotel closer to Palm Beach, where they had relocated, Shannon couldn't believe the changes she and Rafe had wrought last night and this morning.

The most dramatic change was to her eyes, their real color now hidden behind brown contact lenses. Next came her hair, which she had darkened from rich chocolate to espresso using a semipermanent dye, then trimmed so that soft bangs fell to the level of her brows and hid her all-too-noticeable bruise. A ponytail and a pair of cheap red plastic glasses, sans corrective lenses, and a matching teal maid's smock and stretch pants completed her transformation.

Exiting the bathroom, she said, "Ta-da!" and twirled around.

"Whoa," said Garrett, looking up from his computer. "That's a different look."

Without further comment, he returned to the work that had commanded his attention throughout much of the night. Still pale and thin and drinking one mug of coffee after the next, Garrett had at least tapered off the pain pills to work on his part of their mission almost around the clock.

While Garrett tapped away, Rafe scrutinized Shannon for several seconds before saying, "Nice disguise. You'll attract a lot less notice. But it's too bad about the pat-down. Otherwise we'd get you some padding for that uniform. That body of yours—there's no disguising those curves."

Shannon suppressed a smile, telling herself she had no business caring whether Rafe Lyons even noticed she was female. And no business, either, thinking about how uncomfortable he had looked, sleeping on that rollaway last night, after he'd insisted on leaving the room's two beds for her and Garrett.

But she would have to get used to the idea that her awareness of the Ranger went far deeper than the physique only partially hidden by the formfitting dark tee and fatigue-style pants he was wearing. Went beyond the powerful athleticism that came through in his movements, the hint of swagger in his speech, and his total focus on his goal, which both drove her crazy and made her want to pry up the edges of his armor to lay her hand atop the grief-bruised heart beneath.

She imagined what such a moment would be like, her mind instantly flooded with the heat of his body, the texture of his coarse chest hair tickling the sides of her fingers. The exhilaration she would feel at the sight of his panther's eyes dilating—just before he flipped her onto her back beneath him, his knee separating her thighs to...

As her mouth went dry, she shook off the image, reminding herself that this brand of distraction would get her nowhere. Nowhere except dead, a destination with an even worse view than this cut-rate hotel room.

"A guy like Powers won't even see me. He'll take one look, if that, at the cheap glasses and the uniform, and poof!" Shannon clicked her fingers. "I'm suddenly invisible. Just another female functionary."

Rafe's expression sobered, and worry creased his forehead. "I hope like hell you're right and we can get this done today."

Shannon made a fist and bumped his arm lightly, for luck, reverting to her inner tomboy, the girl so many guys saw as their friend, a member of the team and not a romantic prospect. But was he really her friend and partner, or her captor—and the man she planned to use before arresting?

"Quiet down, you two. I'm almost...almost in the system." The clattering of Garrett's fingers across the keyboard intensified, his healing left arm better able to do its part after a couple of days.

Along with Rafe, Shannon turned, her breath held as she focused on the sweat dripping from Garrett's face. Their entire plan, their every hope, could so easily collapse now. If his intrusion triggered any alarms in the remote system he was breaching, the professionals monitoring it would yank it offline in a heartbeat. And once Powers—who was infamous for his paranoia, according to what Rafe had told her—caught wind of it, he would lock down the premises while he packed up his people and his property, and disappeared....

Both Rafe and Shannon hurried to look over his shoulder at a black screen overlaid with scrolling lines of text. As far as Shannon was concerned, it was all Greek, but Rafe grunted his approval and explained, "Now all you have to do is manually plug the flash drive into Powers's firewalled system to introduce the code to get us full control."

Garrett murmured some explanation about rootkits and backdoors that Shannon decided she didn't need to understand, so she concentrated instead on those matters that impacted her directly. "I still don't quite understand how this is going to get you in, Rafe."

"The management company renting Powers's villa— apparently it's poor form to just go ahead and call them mansions—uses automated home systems—networked computers—to control their properties' climate, water, electrical and security systems. These are all monitored

24/7 from a remote location. Once the subroutine kicks in on Powers's system, Garrett can use the management company's server—which he's just hacked into—to cause all sorts of mayhem in Powers's rental."

"So why couldn't you introduce this virus over the internet? In fact, I've been wondering why you or your hacker friends can't get into Powers's personal computer that way and come up with his records on the adoption transaction."

"First of all," Rafe said, "we think he's keeping only written records."

Garrett nodded before offering the real explanation. "And if we could get into the computer on his property, we would, believe me. But the U.S. government could learn a thing or two from the pro who secured Powers's in-house system. There are so many layers of protection, it's a miracle we ever put together who Powers was in the first place. But at least Rafe's learned where the automated home portal is in the house, so you can manually infect the firewall."

She nodded. "So how will you know whether or not I've succeeded?"

"The minute we have access, I'll hear a ping on this end," Garrett said.

Rafe nodded. "And after Garrett wreaks his havoc, I'll be giving Powers a call—using an internet-based spoofing site to make it look like I'm calling from Secure Solutions, the company responsible for monitoring the villa. I'll apologize for the problem and offer to come personally to oversee the repair. And that'll get me inside."

"And me, too," Garrett insisted, though this had never been part of the plan.

"We'll talk about that later," Rafe assured him, though *no* was in his eyes.

"This all sounds great," said Shannon, "*if* I can get in without anyone discovering the flash drive. And *if* Powers doesn't insist on someone he knows coming in to fix the problem." Her stomach squirmed with the thought of so many ifs....

As she took in the tension radiating from Garrett and the worry in Rafe's face, she had to remind herself repeatedly that at the end of the day, she couldn't allow any of this morning's goals to matter more to her than her sworn duty to bring in the AWOL Ranger the moment this was over.

THOUGH SHE TRIED TO HIDE IT, Rafe caught the ripple of tension in Shannon's voice as she glanced over at the digital clock and said, "Van's leaving the lot pretty soon, so how 'bout that lift now, cowboy?"

Good to know he wasn't the only one feeling so jumpy that he was ready to claw his way out of his own skin.

"Wouldn't miss it for the world," he said, ignoring her eyes to focus on her mouth, those beautiful, full lips. Lips that triggered far too many fantasies—impossible delusions brought on by their forced proximity these past few days.

Ten minutes later they reached the parking lot of a down-at-the-heels strip mall. The blue van he'd been told to look for hadn't shown up yet, so they settled in to wait, sipping at the *cafes con leche* they had picked up from the drive-through window of a bustling local coffee shop.

"You going to be okay?" he asked.

She shrugged, her manner flippant. "Why wouldn't

I be? I'm just about to go into a situation that could get me fired—if it doesn't get me killed."

She might think she had him fooled, but Rafe had to wonder, was she really up for this? And did he have any business sending her in?

He swallowed hard, guilt snagging at the hard lump in his throat.

"Wish me luck." One corner of her mouth quirked, forming a perfect dimple in her cheek. A dimple he pictured himself softly kissing.

He scowled, needing to wipe the flippant look from her face, to make her understand how critical this moment was. Looking across the front seat at her, he said, "This is it, Shannon. This means…everything. *She* means everything."

Her eyes softening, she nodded. "I know she does, Rafe," she said. Laying her hand atop his, she gave him a reassuring squeeze.

He closed his eyes, his heartbeat picking up speed at the silken texture of her skin against his, the smooth flesh he had felt, however briefly, when he'd moved her unconscious body. And everything in him yearned to believe what she was telling him, to trust that the woman he had kidnapped and coerced into working for him truly shared his commitment to what would be the final mission of his life.

Still, a question lingered, ghosting to the surface no matter how many times he'd tried to bury it these past few days. Could she only be feigning the compassion he sensed, waiting for her chance to jump out of the cleaning service van and make her break for freedom?

He felt her lean over the console an instant before her unexpected kiss lit the powder keg of his confusion. As he turned to wrap an arm around her, to drag her even closer, moist heat exploded, mouth to mouth and man to woman. Impossibly sensual and tasting of the milky coffee she had been drinking, her lips invited him to linger, to explore the pleasure coursing through him, to use his hands to test curves that had tormented him each night since he'd first set eyes on her.

But as much as Rafe would have liked to taste, to touch, to break the unbearable tension for a short time, he pushed her away, his brain reminding him of the business at hand and his heart's blood going ice-cold with suspicion.

Is Special Agent Shannon Brandt trying to get me so worked up I won't notice that she's kissing me goodbye?

He fought to feign indifference, though his libido was setting off red alerts throughout his system. "We don't have time for fun and games," he snapped in his struggle to get a handle on his frustration.

Surprise flashed over Shannon's face, with hectic spots of color appearing on her cheeks. Only seconds later she shrugged off her clearly hurt feelings—or at least pretended to. "Guess it's true what they say, then, about girls who wear glasses. Well, here's my ride, anyway. See ya later, cowboy."

Without meeting his eyes, she bailed out and walked away from the Yukon—from him—her shoulders hunched as if she were fending off a freezing wind rather than a balmy eighty-degree morning.

As she headed for the van, with its complement of older cleaning women, Rafe was gripped by an urge to go after her, to drag her back to the SUV and sort out what he—what both of them—were feeling. But as he reached for the door handle, a memory slammed him full-force—a vision of Lissa laughing, her hand resting so lovingly on the swollen mound of life that formed her belly.

It was the last photo she had sent him, the last picture taken of his little sister before the attack that left both her face and body too brutalized to allow for an open-casket funeral. One final, sacred image seared into his brain....

Moving his hand back to the steering wheel, he blew out a deep breath and watched Shannon climb into the blue van. Watched and waited several minutes until Rodriguez Cleaning and its newest employee pulled back into traffic and turned in the direction of the oceanside mansions of Palm Beach.

Chapter Ten

Twenty minutes later Shannon was sitting in the van and struggling with the memory of the impulse, as insane as it had been irresistible, that had prompted her to kiss Rafe Lyons. What on earth had been wrong with her? Was she scared, attracted—or, worse yet, actively trying to sabotage her last chance at redemption? Because nothing except loss and heartbreak upon heartbreak could possibly come of a romantic entanglement with a man who had already broken so many laws. A man who would likely end up imprisoned for life.

If he didn't end up dead instead.

Same as you will if Powers and his men see through this disguise....

Wrinkling her nose, she crushed out the unwanted thought like one of her uncle's smelly cigars. Because she wasn't about to die here—or prove her brother right.

This life's not for you, sis. You try to act tough, but I know you. You want to set down roots, not move from place to place with every new assignment. You want to raise a couple of nice kids and maybe a few horses, not chase after drug traffickers and bank robbers all your life.

Looking down at her with his eyes the color of worn

denim, he had even added, *And there's not a damned thing wrong with any of that.*

She ground her teeth at the thought, the insult that he thought her just another quitter, a woman so weak she would toss away the badge she'd worked so hard for, the heritage she clung to, for the kind of life *he* thought she ought to lead just because it was safe.

Unless… Was that really what he'd meant, or had she read more into Steve's comments than he had been saying? What if, instead of spewing contempt, her older brother had really been trying to give her his blessing to do whatever would make her happy, without regard for the family "heritage"?

My career, if I still have one. That's all I want now. Isn't it?

The fluid Spanish conversation she had tuned out stopped abruptly, and both of the graying women sitting with her turned to eye her coldly. Had she let a curse slip, or a whispered snatch of prayer? Looking from one dark gaze to the next, Shannon tried to ferret out the nature of their disapproval.

Though she couldn't understand the words, she recognized the sharp and scolding tone in the warning coming from the driver—a tiny woman with a mass of steely curls who had introduced herself as Señor Rafe's *amiga*, Paloma Rodriguez. When the women's talk resumed, the anxiety accenting their whispers was as universal as the terror in their glances.

Had Paloma, nervous as she was, just told the other women who she really was and why she was there?

Shannon's heart stuttered, her stomach clenching with the dread that one or more of these women—who were housekeepers, not trained operatives—was bound to give her away, either intentionally or accidentally. Why on earth had Paloma risked sharing her secret with them rather than using the cover story Rafe had given her?

But it was too late to abort now, too late to do anything but pray as they turned onto a street lined with slender palms and mansions that ranged from the quietly tasteful to the loudly extravagant. Before Shannon could wonder which one housed a killer, they pulled up to a gate so elegantly wrought it might have graced a castle. Flanking it, two lantern-hung posts gave way to thick white-blossom-studded hedges that tastefully shrouded solid walls. Those walls, she imagined, stood only on the street side, leaving the front of the house open to the nearly fourteen-million-dollar ocean view.

From the pillow where she perched to see over the steering wheel, Paloma Rodriguez cranked down the front window, then stabbed at a keypad with a trembling pudgy finger. Moments later a green light winked and she chirruped, "Rodriguez Cleaning. *B-buenos días.*"

Hyperaware of the woman's nervous stammer, Shannon tensed, preparing to slide open the side door and take off running if she had to.

"Mornin', Paloma." The male voice from the speaker sounded more bored than suspicious. With a regal slowness, the double gates yawned inward, and the blue van rolled onto the tropically landscaped property.

Releasing a long breath, Shannon forced spring-loaded muscles to stand down and took in the flagstone drive that opened to a view of a magnificent Mediterranean-style villa. Enormous yet elegant, its golden brown exterior was inset with a row of blue-and-white Italian tile and capped by a red roof. The graceful, repeated flow of arches, the riot of color from the flaming blooms of Royal Poinciana trees, and the huge hanging baskets spilling with equally flamboyant bougainvillea, formed a feast for eyes raised on the softer palette of the northern latitudes, especially with the Atlantic rippling behind it, a glistening blue mirror beneath the morning sun.

But Shannon wasn't there to goggle at the mansion or the obscenely expensive foreign cars, from sleek Italian roadsters to a Maserati to a big, black Bentley, parked along the semicircular drive. Especially not when she was certain that every one of them had been bought with the blood of innocents—blood that Dominic Powers had ordered spilled for…what? A swanky address and some shiny hunks of metal? The thought of how much they'd cost in suffering made her almost wish she'd ignored Rafe's instructions to smuggle in a weapon so she could put a quick and permanent stop to this evil herself.

She reminded herself that Powers's death, however justified, might not stop the machine he'd set in motion, nor would it return the stolen infants to their biological families. *Focus on the mission.* As the van parked beside what appeared to be a service entrance, the mantra worked its magic, as it had so many times when she had taken part in officially sanctioned operations.

Taking her cue from her fellow housekeepers, she climbed out and grabbed a dust mop and squirt bottle from the back, then lined up single file at the door. Mindful of the flash drive she had carefully hidden in her ponytail, she mentally braced herself for a body search and prayed they would never think of looking anywhere above her neckline.

Two men strolled outside, their barrel chests puffed out, their brown eyes predatory. White males in their mid-thirties, the pair looked so similar they must have been brothers, maybe even twins, with their blocky faces and hands that looked as if they could crush women's throats for sport. Only an inch or two taller than Shannon's five-seven, their weight lifters' builds and broad faces made them appear far larger. But it was the pair of chinstrap beards—thin strips of coarse hair accentuating powerful jaws—that sent up neon flares of alarm. Because the meticulously trimmed beards, one reddish and the other dark brown, matched the witness descriptions of the murderers seen climbing from plumbing vans in three states.

What morons, not to shave them. No, not stupid, she warned herself, as she noticed how intently she was being studied. They had to be intelligent, not simply well-trained, to have pulled off so many murders without getting caught or killed. Just vain, which explained both their failure to change their facial hair and the expensive cut of the tropical linen suits they wore, the ridiculous rich man's shoes making a statement of their feet.

Though it defied both her nature and her instinct, she dropped her gaze in an attempt to look subservient and—especially—uninteresting.

"What's this?" the one with the red beard demanded.

Paloma raised her graying head to answer. *"Mi sobrina*—my niece. She work with me this summer. Need the extra money."

"But the summer's almost over," Brown Beard said with a shake of his head before his wide jaw split in a disturbing grin. "Where you been hidin' this little *chiquita* up 'til now?"

With that he held up the metal-detecting wand he was carrying and sketched one half of an hourglass shape beside her body. "Might have to search you a little more thoroughly inside, *mamacita.*"

With his brother hooting encouragement, all four

women froze, waves of tension rolling from them like the ocean lapping at the shore. With the memory of the crime scene photos from Lissa Smith's murder flashing before her eyes, Shannon managed a stiff, "I'm here to work. Clean this place."

Red Beard's laughter stopped abruptly, as if someone had cut it off with a knife. "You speak English real good, little mama."

There was a threatening edge in his voice, an edge that warned her that her hope to go unnoticed had failed miserably.

Really well, *you mean?* But she kept the thought to herself, knowing her best chance was to conform to these men's stereotypes. "Thank you," she said quietly. "I been in Florida my whole life. Do good work cleaning houses."

"Bet you do your best work in the bedroom, don'tcha, sweetie?" whooped the darker-bearded brother as, sure enough, he searched her, not even bothering to disguise the fact that he was feeling her up in the process.

Face flaming, Shannon shook, not with fear as much as the wish she'd brought Rafe's stun gun—or possibly his AK-47. *Lyons, you seriously owe me.*

"Come inside with me," the jerk said when he finished. "and I'll show you an easier way to make a lot more money than you'll get on your hands and knees."

"Don't believe him," Red Beard laughed. "He'll have you on your hands and knees before you know what hit you."

He was interrupted by a beep from his phone. After frowning down at the screen, he said, "Party's over, *señoritas.* Looks like it's gonna be business before pleasure after all."

As they filed inside, Brown Beard couldn't resist swatting Shannon's behind and saying, "Why don't you start with polishing my toilet, baby. If I happen by, you be sure'n hold the seat up for me...."

As the men left, cracking up at their own wit, Shannon followed Paloma and the other women, and fumed quietly. *I am* so *going to look the other way while Rafe leaves nothing of you losers but a pair of greasy splotches.*

After taking several deep breaths to cool her temper, she watched the other two women slip off to their respective duties, their heads bowed as if in shame. She followed the tiny figure of Paloma Rodriguez, watching as the woman looked furtively about a beautifully appointed kitchen littered with half-eaten take-out food and empty wine bottles, before passing Shannon a folded half sheet of paper she extracted from the pocket of her smock.

"You go here," she said, pointing a stubby finger at a roughly penciled map with an *X* marking the room Shannon presumed must be the study. "You find what you need there. Be quick and careful as you can. *El Jefe,* the big boss, he go there many times to make calls and write things in that book he carry. But maybe not this early. He party late, sleep long. Best days are when we go before he wake up."

Shannon took a few steps in the direction of the study before she hesitated, turning. "You mean he's even *worse* than those two?"

Paloma nodded, her dark eyes clearly frightened. "Oh, *sí. Los dos*—those two—they just play with us, like *el tigre* toying with the rabbit when his belly full already. But Señor Powers—" her voice dropped to a whisper "—he take what he like, when he like. No because he not have other women, fancy ladies from his parties, but because he like to taste fear. This is why I stop bringing the young girls to clean, especially my daughters."

Wonderful. If Shannon had known things were this bad, she definitely would have found a way to at least stick on a couple of big, hairy fake moles and a gray wig while she was at it.

"Then why would you keep coming?" Though she shouldn't waste the time, Shannon couldn't shake the suspicion that the question needed asking. That in some way or another her life might depend upon the answer. Lowering her voice even further, she touched the woman's trembling hand and said, "If what you say is true, you could have that man arrested."

The gray curls shook; the eyes beneath them lowered. "I cannot because he know. He know people who make *mi familia* leave this country and return to Cuba."

"What else do I need to know, Paloma?"

"No. No more talk." The older woman gave Shannon a slight push. "You go now. Go and take care of this business."

Doubt crawling up the back of her throat, Shannon hesitated, torn between the hope that Paloma was using her and Rafe to defuse a dangerous threat and the worry that the older woman might try to curry favor or cave in to her fears by telling *El Señor* about his dangerous intruder. One last time, Shannon pressed. "For your daughters, your *bebés,* please…"

Shannon had only meant to strengthen her appeal, but at her mention of the Spanish word for "babies," Paloma jerked back, looking as though she had been slapped hard across the face.

"No—no, *señorita,*" she pleaded. "You must never

mention *bebés*—ever. Must never speak to them or even look while you are here."

Shannon blinked, shocked almost speechless by what she was hearing. "You mean—you mean they're bringing babies *here?*" she whispered. "To this villa? *Where,* Paloma? Where does he keep the little ones?"

"Go." Once more Paloma pushed her, her panic careening toward hysteria. "You go now, or everything off."

Shannon pinned the tiny woman with a look. "You say one word to him about me or my—my associate, your problems with *Inmigración* are just beginning, understand me? We're with the federal government, and we can make things worse—or *you* can choose to make them better."

With a pang of guilt about the need to treat Paloma so harshly, Shannon headed in the direction the maid's map had indicated. Alert for the bearded brothers, Powers or any guests or staff, she resisted the impulse to finger the thick ponytail where the tiny device lay hidden—so simple in appearance but so crucial to their plans.

She reminded herself that all she had to do was get to the security computer and plug the flash into the USB drive so she could launch it. Once she succeeded, her part would be finished, and all Rafe expected her to do was look busy until she could leave with the other women.

Unless she spotted any sign of children on the premises…. Maybe Powers really had been bringing them here while he milked top dollar from competing potential adopters. An electric current of excitement coursed through her as she imagined laying Lissa's stolen child into Rafe's strong arms, then smiling up to see that warrior's face soften. Fleeting as it was, the familylike image stole into her heart—until she had to force herself to imagine cuffing Rafe the moment he passed the baby to Garrett….

It was what she had promised herself. *So why does it hurt so badly to imagine?*

Swallowing hard, she put it out of mind and focused on a mansion that seemed to go on forever. Consulting her map at intervals, she hurried through numerous arched portals, passing elegant, artfully scattered furnishings, sparkling chandeliers and delicate-looking, translucent vases that stood on pedestals illuminated from above by tiny spotlights. And everywhere, a huge aquamarine pool just outside and, farther out, the azure ocean blazed their brilliant blues beyond walls of windows, a brilliance that drew the eye and softly whispered *hurry* with each wavelet breaking on the sugary-white beach.

One large sitting area stopped her in her tracks. Or the gallery of photos did, each an oversize, soft-focus depiction of some of the most sacred moments of family life. A grown man's cupped hands, cradling a tiny infant. A young mother curled into a softly moon-lit rocker, her smile gentle and her arms filled with the baby she was feeding. A couple walking along the beach at sunset, a tiny toddler swinging between their joined hands, her bare feet swinging in the surf. Even Shannon, who knew the beautifully made series was meant to manipulate and exploit, couldn't help but feel a tug of primal longing, a lump forming in her throat. Or maybe that was sadness at this all-too-poignant reminder of the joy that had been stolen so ruthlessly from some couples, all of them middle-class or poorer, to be sold to the wealthy.

"So where're you stashing those babies, you heartless

monster? And where's that ledger of yours?" she murmured, before reminding herself that her first priority had to be doing her part to get Rafe inside the villa.

Along the curved corridor leading toward the master suite, she finally found the study, an aggressively masculine room that smelled of old leather and heavy, oiled furnishings, each one darkly gleaming. In keeping with the British aristocrat theme, the windows were hung with heavy draperies. But these at least were practical in nature, cutting the glare on the flat-screened computer system left running on the desktop.

At least she thought it was running, judging from the glowing green button on the front. The screen, however, was dark. In sleep mode, she suspected.

As she closed the door behind her, she caught sight of her own strangely dark eyes in the mirror right beside it. Turning toward the computer, she prayed this really was the central terminal that ran the household systems. *Only one way to find out.*

Her stomach quivering, she reached behind her head. Instead of finding the hard plastic flash drive she had so carefully placed inside her ponytail, she felt absolutely nothing. Nothing but the band binding the silky tail of her hair.

Oh, no. I can't have lost it.

Face burning and heart pounding, she pulled the hair band free and ran her trembling fingers through her unbound locks. Faster than the speed of fear, thoughts streaked through her mind. Had the flash drive fallen as she'd been "searched"? No, the brothers would have seen it and pounced on her in an instant. What about in the van? Or had it happened in the kitchen? Was it somewhere between there and this room? And, once found, would anyone connect it to her?

Of course they will. These men were professionals, not idiots, as much as she would rather believe the latter. Although they might not guess the flash drive's purpose, it would not take long for someone to connect it to the only new person to intrude upon their usual morning routine. Especially a new "toy" whose harassment had given the two sociopaths so much pleasure.

She squatted down, sweeping her hand across the oriental rug in the room's center in the desperate hope the drive had merely dropped when she'd removed the band. Acutely aware that every moment she spent increased the odds she would be caught, she crawled over every step she had taken since entering the room.

Click.

As she cleared the rug's fringed border, plastic bounced off hardwood as the flash drive, which had apparently been caught inside her collar, finally fell from her neckline to the floor. With a sigh louder than the ocean's, she grabbed the flat, two-inch stick and hurled herself toward the computer.

Finding an open USB port, she fumbled to fit the drive into the slot. It slid smoothly home, and she thought she heard—or imagined she heard—some process whirring in the hard drive, though the screen remained obstinately dark.

Desperate for some sign her action had had some effect and that she'd picked the right computer, she nudged the mouse with a single finger. Color filled the screen, the bright red of a stoplight. A single dialogue box, labeled PASSWORD, begged for an entry, while hovering just above it, a countdown screen ticked off the seconds.

29, 28, 27…

Heart racing, Shannon froze. If the countdown made it all the way to zero without her correctly entering the password, would the system simply return to its sleeping state? Or would an alarm shriek throughout the villa, bringing the bearded brothers, their even more dangerous employer and heaven only knew how many other security staffers down like a brick wall on her head?

21, 20, 19…

Rather than trying common passwords, attempts that might in themselves trigger an alarm, Shannon decided her best—her only—option was to put as much distance between herself and this room as she could, preferably moving close to the entrance where the van was. No, too far, she realized. That was the first place they would come looking. Was there another exit, even a window she could unlock?

13, 12…

Rushing toward the door, she flung it open and blasted through so quickly that the shape at her left was no more than a blur. Grabbing her by the waist, strong arms slung her around and held her tight against a strong body. A male body, she realized, as the coldest voice she'd ever heard wormed its way into her ear.

"Where do you think you're going in such a blasted hurry?"

She froze, her gaze shooting through the open office door to the bloodred monitor straight ahead. To the relentless march of numbers, counting off her final seconds…

3, 2, 1...

Loud and shrill, a screech broke the silence of the
household. A screech as piercing as a dying woman's
scream.

Chapter Eleven

Chafing at the interminable wait, Rafe, now dressed in a neat gray uniform made to match those in photos from Secure Solutions' website, checked his watch against the hotel room's digital clock and cursed under his breath.

Garrett turned from where he was sitting at the desk with his laptop. "Would you please knock that off?"

"Knock what off?" A few off-color words ought to be the least of either of their worries.

The smaller man shot Rafe his most annoyed look. "Are you kidding? The sighing, the pacing, the bugging me about whether we're still in the system. I thought *I* was the rookie here and you do this sort of thing twice before breakfast every day of the week."

"Not quite—and this is different. I know Paloma said the computer in the study's the one that stays with every renter, but what if she was wrong? What if they're running the villa from some control closet she's never set eyes on?"

"That's not really what's bothering you, is it?" Garrett studied him, his gray eyes so clear and focused, Rafe could almost believe he really had gotten his head together and his priorities sorted, as he'd claimed.

"I'm worried about why that damned computer hasn't pinged yet."

"Admit it. You're really worried about Shannon."

Rafe scowled, then resumed his pacing, hating the confines of a room too cramped to contain his energy. Peering past the curtain into the parking lot below, he shook his head. "What if she never even showed up? She could've talked Paloma into dropping her somewhere. Somewhere she could call in the cavalry to lead a raid on us here at any second."

"If she were planning to escape, wouldn't she have done it days ago? Hell, Rafe, she could have shot us in our sleep."

"She's not the type. But when it comes down to a by-the-book betrayal—"

Garrett frowned. "Like she said, she really wants a piece of stopping Powers, not us. Probably dreaming of the fat promotion she'll get for pulling off the biggest bust of her career. But that's not what you're worried about. You're worried about *her*. With Powers. Listen, man, I'm not blind. I've seen the way you look at her when you think no one's watching."

"Of course I'm keeping an eye on her. Why wouldn't I, when everything hinges on her part in—"

"It's more than that. Come on, man."

Rafe shrugged. "Yeah, so she's one good-looking woman, sleeping in the same room with us. Who wouldn't have noticed?"

"You like her. Really like her."

"What is this, junior high school?" Rafe gestured irritably toward the computer. "Why the devil hasn't that thing beeped yet?"

Because they've killed her. Because Paloma's sold us all out. Maybe Powers has known we're coming after him for days—since before his goons tried to roast us out of that motel room.

Maybe he'd been wrong in his assumption that Powers's men would have handled a hit far more professionally than the amateur-hour attacker Shannon had taken out. Maybe lethally wrong—with Shannon paying the price right now for his mistake.

The computer's high-pitched ping nearly stopped his heart.

"It really worked. She did it!" Garrett cried, jumped from his seat to pump his fist.

"She's alive," Rafe said, his eyes closing as he breathed a prayer of thanks. Or at least she had survived long enough to pop the viral payload into the right USB port.

"Time for a little mayhem." Garrett rubbed his hands together, sounding almost giddy as he began tapping at his keyboard, using the remote connection to hijack the now-vulnerable brain of Powers's rented automated home.

"Power's down," he reported, his foot tapping out his nervous tension. "Now the water, and finally, the coup de grâce—the backup power for his security systems. Okay, Rafe. You're on."

With his heart hammering and anxiety clawing his gut, it was all Rafe could do not to initiate his spoofed call right that second. To take another step toward learning whether Shannon had not only performed her role but managed to survive it.

But it was time to stuff down his emotions, to think like the team leader and the elite soldier he was. "Let's give Powers a minute to take notice and get worked up. The more pissed off he gets, the less control he's going to have." And the less clearly he would be thinking.

But Rafe didn't dare wait too long, giving Powers or one of his men time to contact the management company. So in precisely sixty seconds—sixty seconds that dragged past at an excruciatingly slow pace—he nodded to Garrett, who initiated the call-spoofing program.

Rafe's phone rang first, and once he answered, the call seamlessly went through to the number the indispensable Paloma had provided. Once, twice, the phone at Powers's villa rang, while Rafe stood still as stone, his legs cemented to the floor by tension. *Check the caller ID and pick up. Pick up. Pick—*

"What the hell is going on?" a furious male voice shouted. "What sort of incompetence—I was *guaranteed* 'seamless integration,' 'flawless delivery,' '24/7 security surveillance,' and what do I get? Is this what you fools call first-class service?"

Powers himself, Rafe realized. Did this callous bastard even know Lissa's name?

Rafe somehow forced himself to respond in a subservient tone that burned his throat like acid. "I apologize, sir. I'm afraid we've encountered a platform conflict while performing a routine upgrade on our—"

"Who *is* this?" Powers demanded, the chill in his voice a palpable force.

"This is Gregor Julian from Secure Solutions," Rafe said, using a name he had seen mentioned in a blog written by the technician. "And speaking personally, I'm truly sorry for the inconvenience." The necessity of groveling to this monster had Rafe shaking with barely suppressed rage. "I can have someone out there to remedy the situation in two or three hours."

There was a brief hesitation before Powers demanded, "Do you have any idea how much this place costs me a month? Do you, *Gregor?*"

I do, you soulless piece of garbage. And what's more,

I know how you came up with the money for your rent.
"I understand you expect impeccable service, and as
soon as our technicians take care of the other customers
on our list—"

Powers's voice cooled from white heat to an even-
more-threatening sub-Arctic in an instant. "I don't give
a damn about your *other* customers. Do you understand
that, you idiot? Screw them over all you want, but if you
aren't here within half an hour, I promise you, I will use
every power at my disposal to see that you personally
pay the price."

"All right, sir," Rafe promised. "I'll come right over
myself. Give me twenty minutes." *Only you're the one
whose bill's come due, Dominic. With interest, once I
have the information I need.*

"I'll be waiting," Powers told him before the line went
dead in his ear.

"This is it," Rafe told Garrett as he reached for the
cap that matched his uniform. "I'm on the move."

Garrett stood, his gaze darting around like a trapped
animal's. "Let me come with you. Please, Rafe. I know
it wasn't in the plan, but I have to see him. I need to
make him pay for what he did to her. To us."

Rafe clapped a hand on Garrett's shoulder, mainly
to still the younger man's frenetic movements. "Stay
here, like we agreed. This isn't the time to deviate from
the—"

"What do I care about the damned plan? All I care
about is seeing that son of a bitch dead. Him and his
two butchers."

He meant it, Rafe understood. Regardless of his
mistakes, his weakness, Garrett really had loved Lissa.
"Don't worry, bro," Rafe assured him. "They *will* pay.
But right now we stick to the plan. Because nothing we

can do, nothing we can say, is ever going to bring back Lissa or those other women. The best thing, the most important thing either of us ever will do in our lives is find every last one of those babies and get them to their rightful homes."

"YOU'RE A VERY FORTUNATE YOUNG WOMAN."

Shannon heard the tall man speaking as if from a great distance. An entire ocean, black as midnight, pitched between her and the fang-sharp iceberg of his voice.

No, that's not right. He's right here, right next to me. Cruel fingers proved it, pinching at the tender flesh inside her elbow so painfully that she gasped, eyes flashing open.

Releasing her bruised arm, Powers smiled down at her where she lay on the floor of the faux-English office where he must have dragged her after choking her unconscious. A face swam into focus, a lean, forty-ish face that might have been handsome, were it not for the smile so soulless and blue eyes so empty that they reminded her of a skull's. Tanned and fit, he was wearing white shorts and a polo shirt, everything spotless and unwrinkled, his wavy, slightly mussed hair the only sign that their brief struggle had ruffled him at all.

Strangely disconnected, a thought skittered across her mind. *So this is what pure evil looks like....*

"How am I *lucky?*" she asked, her voice so hoarse and distant it might have been a stranger's. "I finish cleaning in here, and you hurt me for no reason."

"*Liar.*" He straightened in one swift movement and brought his heel down, aiming for the fingers of her left hand.

Snatching them clear, Shannon tried to roll away to

escape, but a second pair of overpriced shoes stopped her. Shoes belonging to the brother with the red beard, who was staring down at her with barely disguised hunger. Staring down the barrel of the big revolver in his hand.

Shuddering, she sat up and wrapped her arms around her body. Her nearly naked body, she realized with a stomach-dropping jolt of horror.

"I'm afraid we had to remove your uniform," Powers explained, as if he'd read her panicked thoughts. "Had to make certain you weren't running from this room with something you had stolen. Or that you haven't come into my home wearing a wire or something equally unfortunate."

"I'm no thief," she assured him, using her hands to shield her bra from his gaze. Crumpled beside her, she spotted the tangle of her discarded clothes and fought the need to grab them, to cover the vulnerability she felt. "And what do you mean, a wire? You mean you think I'm some kind of—"

"You're fortunate we didn't find one," Powers said, "though we haven't yet checked *everywhere*." His stare held such lascivious intent that it left no doubt what sort of search he was suggesting. "Unless you wish to deprive us of that pleasure by confessing first?"

"Confessing what? I haven't done anything!" she cried, scooting a few inches nearer to the uniform. "Where's my aunt Paloma?"

"My other associate is sending those shriveled hens home for the day—and putting the fear of God into them while he's at it." Powers pulled out the desk chair, sat down and crossed his legs. "Then he'll be back to help us get some answers from you. And believe me, he and his brother are well-versed in persuasion."

She thought about the women they'd killed, of the measureless cruelty they must possess to commit such horrible acts. Were they hurting Paloma even now for lying about her?

"Answers to what?" she asked.

"Answers about the power and security outage that oh-so-coincidentally began within moments after I caught you bolting from this room."

Shannon shook her head in feigned confusion. "What makes you think I know anything about that?"

"Perhaps you should take a look in the mirror," he invited, reaching down to grab her by the neck and hair before hauling her to her feet, "and ask yourself that very question."

Red Beard took her arm, and the two men dragged her to a little oval mirror hanging by the door. A mirror from which her own terrified eyes stared back, one eye dark brown and the other her natural icy blue. Her heart sagged, knowing one contact must have popped off during her struggle with Powers.

Leaning toward her, his face contorting, shifting into something hideous, Powers asked, "Who are you working with?"

"Working with?" she echoed. "Rodriguez Clean—"

She hadn't finished the lie before Red Beard slammed a fist into her lower back. The pain was so severe, so sudden, she couldn't even scream. Though her knees gave way, he held her upright, pulling her close against a body that betrayed his excitement.

"Once more, to the kidneys," the ice-cold voice directed, and the man with the red beard all-too-eagerly complied. "Now the rib cage. No, not the face. It's rather pretty, and I do enjoy a nice view when I'm between a girl's legs."

Shannon found herself lying on the floor again, pain an endless detonation in the places where she had been struck. Worse was the terror that he would make good on his threat to rape her, that the bearded man would join him, and perhaps his brother, too. Somehow she had to regain control, not only of her body but of this situation.

Powers settled in a nearby chair, then leaned down. "Did that improve your memory? Or what about this?" He held the flash drive between two fingers, the drive that she had left in the back of the computer. "Who sent you?"

"No one," she whimpered, thinking that whatever they did to her, she wasn't giving up Rafe's or Garrett's name. "I—I came here on my own."

"Then who is this man calling himself Gregor Julian?"

"Who?" The name meant nothing to her, even after Red Beard delivered a hard kick that struck the outside of her knee. Crying out with the pain, she said, "I don't know—I swear it."

"He's your partner, isn't he?" Powers asked. "The fool claiming he's with Secure Solutions? As if I would think nothing of his calling me on the house line rather than my personal cell number, as the company's representatives have in the past."

Despair washed over her, striking in wave after wave even stronger than the agony of her injuries. Not Rafe, too... She had to think of some way to keep Powers and his men from killing him the moment he set foot in this death trap. "Maybe this Mr. Julian is new. Or maybe—"

"You're together in this, aren't you? What I need to

know—what you most certainly will tell me—is who you both really are, and what the devil you want."

She thought of claiming her true identity, but he would never buy the idea of an FBI agent showing up alone, unarmed, without even the scant protection of a wire. And she knew instinctively that betraying any knowledge of the stolen infants would quickly get her killed.

So what, then, could she use to throw him off completely?

"I'm telling you the truth. I've never heard of this guy, or Secure Solutions, either," she insisted, then in a flash of inspiration added, "I only came to copy the files, but the minute I touched it, your computer started going crazy."

"My files?" Powers's voice dropped to sub-zero. "What files?"

"Financial records," she continued improvising, thinking only of pulling Powers's suspicions a little further off track. "Th-they're offering good money."

"Who is?" Dropping to his knees, Powers seized her by the arm and glared into her face. "Don't make me drag this out of you, or I swear you'll regret it."

"The IRS," she said, naming the one agency most Americans, even criminals, found more frightening than the FBI and CIA combined. "They're looking for proof you're cheating on your taxes."

"The IRS? You—you're saying that they pay informants? That you're some kind of IRS mole?"

"A *snitch*." Red Beard's mouth twisted, uttering the word as if it were the vilest curse. "I *hate* snitches."

"I'm not a snitch, I'm more of a bounty hunter…kind of." Jerking her arm free of Powers's grasp, she snatched her discarded pants off the floor. "Except I bring back files and they make their own arrest."

"Why would the IRS think I'm some common tax cheat—?" Powers sounded ridiculously offended for someone who murdered trophy wives and expectant mothers to pad his bank accounts.

"They didn't say why." Feigning nonchalance despite her pain and terror, Shannon thrust a foot into one pant leg. "They never tell me that much, but a lot of things can tip them off. An angry business rival. Weird write-offs. Or maybe you've forgotten to file your returns for five years." Flinging one arm out in a frantic gesture to encompass the huge villa, she added, "Or how about living a whole lot larger than your reported means?"

"Surely the IRS doesn't imagine I'm stupid enough to keep evidence of something like this lying about on a computer that runs the outdoor sprinklers and dims the lights at bedtime. Or was that *your* brilliant idea?"

She finished wriggling into the pants, gaining confidence with every square inch of her flesh she covered. "How am I supposed to know one computer from another? All I'm trained to do is copy spreadsheets, and I never even got a peek at the hard drive of your stupid, booby-trapped computer."

Red Beard shook his blocky head. "Since when does the IRS go around hiring snitches?"

"Bounty hunters," she corrected once more, grunting with pain while reaching for the teal smock. "And I'm telling you, the IRS rewards are awesome—you wouldn't believe how much they're willing to pay when they're slavering after some fat-cat tax cheat. No offense, of course."

"Of course," Powers echoed drily.

"But if somebody else, say, were to offer me a

better deal…" popping her head through the neck opening, Shannon infused her voice with a wheedling tone "…then a girl might possibly be persuaded to sub in another set of data. One the federal prosecutors would find completely useless."

"I cannot believe this," Powers muttered, his voice dripping with scorn. "You not only expect me to let you go, you expect me to pay you off while I'm at it?"

"For ten—let's make it twelve—grand, I can disappear, throw 'em off of your trail for months."

"Twelve thousand dollars? For sneaking into my home and attempting to steal from me?"

"For medical costs," she said, scraping together one last ration of pure chutzpah. "A real bargain for the gentleman wanting to avoid a lot of messy charges. False imprisonment, assault…and I imagine it'd be real hard joining the local yacht club if you had to register as some sort of pervy sex offender for the rest of your life on account of those threats you made."

Red Beard snorted, his disgust abruptly turning to amusement. "Cost you a lot less to let me haul her down to the marina, then dump her a few miles offshore, boss. And we could have ourselves a little party on the yacht first, *snitch*."

Shannon rolled her eyes and scoffed, "You're kidding. Truly. You think those IRS guys don't know where they sent me? Trust me, you do not want those people up your rear ends, turning this place inside-out and looking into every dime you ever made in your life."

Something in the room buzzed, and Powers, looking both perplexed and disconcerted, fished a cell phone from the pocket of his pockets. "Yes? Oh, he's here? Check him thoroughly. And the vehicle, as well, and, Karl…I'll need you to put a call through to Secure

Solutions. Check to see if Gregor Julian has come back to work for them."

Shannon's heart thumped wildly. Would this be the moment when things fell to pieces? The moment when both she and Rafe were lost?

As Powers disconnected, he looked her over as if she were no more than some particularly fascinating insect—one to study one last time before he crushed it underfoot.

Chapter Twelve

"Someone just called to see if you were still working with Secure Solutions," said Garrett, who'd intercepted the call and routed it to his phone through the hijacked system. "I assured them you're our best, but let me warn you. They're practically foaming at the mouth about the trouble we caused."

"We've got bigger problems," Rafe said in the direction of his cell phone, which he'd set on speaker before laying it on the seat of the white van he was driving. Just after leaving the rental company lot, he had carefully applied a magnetized Secure Solutions sign he'd had made days ago in preparation for this moment.

"They've already let you in the gate, right?" Garrett's voice sounded worried.

"I'm in, all right." Rafe scanned the villa's exterior and its lush surroundings. "But the Rodriguez Cleaning van's not here."

"Thought they always worked 'til noon. It's only... I've got ten-forty."

"Yeah," Rafe said uneasily, watching for the security team he was expecting any second. "And Paloma hasn't called to check in like she promised. Which makes me wonder if someone's given her a very good reason to keep her mouth shut."

"No contact here from Shannon, either. Maybe you should pull out. I've got a very bad feeling about—" Garrett was interrupted by a loud banging, a noise that sounded as if it was coming from inside his room at the hotel.

"What's that?" Rafe asked him, just as the villa's service entrance opened. Two men strode his way, the first tattooed, olive-skinned and possibly Hispanic. But it was the other who commanded Rafe's attention. Dark-bearded, stocky, white. Could he be one of the pair who had murdered Lissa?

As the two men drew near, Rafe forced himself to put his sister's killing out of his mind, to focus on rescue instead of retribution. As the pair drew close enough for him to make out their hard eyes and hostile faces, he wondered, were they braced for confrontation or, like a pair of pit bulls with spike collars and cropped ears, merely sent to intimidate all who set foot on this property? How many others like them did Powers keep around?

"Someone's at the door," Garrett answered just before what sounded like a muffled male voice bled through the speaker, a shouted *"Open it!"* followed by something Rafe could not make out.

Alarm spiked through him. "Who is it? Garrett?"

"I have to go now."

"Don't hang up," Rafe said, worried even more by the persistent hammering he had heard than what he saw heading his way. Then he heard another sound. A louder bang? A gunshot? A door splintering as someone kicked it open?

"Garrett?" But it was too late. The line had gone dead, leaving Rafe with no idea whether his brother-in-law was being arrested, robbed or even murdered.

Tension fisted in his gut, but with the men bearing down on him, he was forced to compartmentalize his emotions. Forced to focus, if he expected to survive to find his niece, returning her to… Furiously, he shook his head. He couldn't think about Garrett's situation right now, couldn't wonder whether his niece would have a living parent.

Gripping the driver's-side door handle, Rafe hesitated one last second, wondering if there was any chance of putting this van in gear and bashing his way through the now-closed gates to speed across town in time to help Garrett. Or did he stick with his original plan of trying to get inside the villa—forcing the issue if need be?

Because his gut told him that Garrett wasn't the only one in danger, that Shannon was still somewhere inside, in the kind of trouble it would take every bit of his commando training, and no small measure of luck, to get her out of alive.

In the end, logistics made his mind up for him. Whatever loyalty he owed Garrett, Rafe was certain that in the twenty minutes it would take him to reach the hotel room, whatever was happening would long be over.

Climbing from the van, he offered his right hand to the bearded thug who had taken the lead, along with what Rafe hoped would pass for a loose-and-easy smile. "Gregor Julian, Secure Solutions. Sorry for your trouble this morning with our system."

"All I can say is you better get things back up in a hurry. Now toss that cell phone on your seat—we don't allow 'em inside."

"Sure." Rafe complied as if the request gave him not a moment's worry.

"Okay, *Julia*," the guard said, feminizing Rafe's assumed name like some two-bit schoolyard bully. "Put down the tool kit, turn around and put your hands against the van so we can search you before the boss decides to take this out on us instead of *you.*"

Rafe felt himself being hurriedly frisked, and none too gently. But not thoroughly enough to find the sheath duct-taped behind his fly. In the macho, homophobic world of hired muscle, few things were as offensive— as downright threatening—as an accusation of checking out another man's goods too thoroughly. It was one weakness Rafe had no qualms about using.

Once he was finished, the bearded man squatted to check a tool kit containing a convincing assortment of items Garrett had suggested. Meanwhile, the tattooed man wanded him using a handheld metal detector... which also failed to pick up the carbon-fiber combat dagger Rafe was trusting with his life.

Though the bearded thug wore a shoulder holster beneath his jacket and his tattooed sidekick had already drawn a handgun, Rafe still figured that with only the slightest of diversions to cover his first move, he stood a decent chance of taking down both men. With the security cameras out, it was unlikely he would be seen, but there was still a danger of direct observation from any of the windows in his line of sight.

Better to get inside first, where he could be certain whether anyone was watching. And where the inevitable bloodstains wouldn't be so quick to draw attention.

As long as they're not mine, he reminded himself firmly, knowing that his own life was far from the most important thing at stake.

AFTER TWISTING HER ARM BEHIND HER, Red Beard marched Shannon past a series of arched doorways along the curving corridor. "While you're locked up good and tight, I want you to sweat out every minute, knowing I'll be doing everything I can to talk the boss into letting me give you the full snitch treatment."

"What was your name again?" asked Shannon, though they both knew she had never heard it in the first place. "I want to make sure we get it right on the indictment."

"You think I give a damn about your threats?" he asked, slamming her face-first against a wall as he pressed his body close behind her and moved his hand from her arm to roughly squeeze her breast.

It was his first mistake, the one she had been waiting for.

Snapping her head backward, she slammed her skull into his face. Grunting in surprise and pain, he jerked away, giving her enough space to swing her elbow, driving it into his throat with crushing force.

Falling back, he went for his revolver, gagging and choking as his dark eyes burned with an animal-like hatred—at the insult of being caught off guard by a woman he'd looked forward to tormenting at his leisure. But the bruised windpipe and Red Beard's bulked-out muscles betrayed him, making him a fraction of a second slower than Shannon. She whirled and snapped her knee upward, striking between his legs in a direct hit.

He went down instantly, retching, but still, Shannon—prompted by the Israeli Special Forces–style hand-to-hand combat training she had received—refused to let up, landing a hard kick against the side of his head before bending down and snatching the gun out of his hand.

She would have shot him if she'd had to, but Red Beard appeared to be down for the count, and even if he hadn't been, gunfire would bring others. Instead she took off, praying she could find an unlocked exit before she ran into more trouble—or the man she had just beaten recovered enough to sound the alarm.

Slowed by her own injuries, her pain severe enough to bleed through the adrenaline that fueled her, she heard a roar behind her, a bellow that made her realize that in her panicked state she'd misjudged his temporary daze for true unconsciousness....

Not to mention that she'd enraged her opponent to the point where he would stop at nothing to repay her for the pain and the humiliation he had been dealt.

She heard the hard slap of his shoes against the marble, the footsteps moving far too fast in her direction. For a bare instant Shannon hesitated, thinking to shoot him the moment he came into view. But one look at the revolver she'd taken—a shot-loaded Taurus Judge that would likely hit her target with a hail of spreading lead but fail to kill from any distance—changed her mind. Bolting for cover, she reached for the door Paloma's map had marked as the master suite—a door she could only pray she wouldn't find locked.

RAFE WAS PANTING HARD, wiping the blood from his carbon blade, then sticking the knife beneath his belt, where he could grab it quickly.

When they had first come in, he had hoped that killing them wouldn't be necessary. But all that ended the moment a push-to-talk call from another security guard informed the bearded man that he had checked Rafe's van's registration and found the vehicle to be a rental.

It's done now, so put it behind you and move forward. And count your blessings that you managed to nail them both—including one of Lissa's killers—before either man got off a shot.

Choosing the tattooed man's Beretta but taking the bearded man's weapon and tucking it next to the knife as a backup, he moved slowly through the villa, alert for any sign that the struggle near the service entrance, at the mansion's far end, had drawn attention.

Rafe tried to stay in the zone, but he was having a far tougher time than on any prior mission. Concern for Shannon vied with fears for Garrett—and the worry that he had just dispatched two men to save a woman who had long since bailed on him and was even now leading the raid that captured Garrett.

Troubling as the thought was, could the news be even worse? Could Shannon already have been killed by Powers and Garrett's death have left his child an orphan?

Weapon held in a two-handed grip before him, Rafe moved from one room to the next, repulsed by the extravagance of the beautiful surroundings. *Hope you enjoyed your taste of heaven while you had it, Powers. Because if I have my way, I'll get everything I need and still have time to make this your day of reckoning.*

He advanced into yet another room, one containing a series of photos he had to force himself to tear his gaze away from. Before he could move on, movement beyond the window to his left drew his attention to a walking side of beef with a shaved head and dark glasses—the same guard who'd been forced by the power outage to manually override and open the front gates.

The man appeared to be patrolling the perimeter now. As he walked beside the pool, the sunlight glinted off his diamond earring as his gaze turned toward the villa. Rafe darted into the curving corridor, hoping he had moved in time to keep the guard from catching sight of him. Praying he could stay clear of trouble for at least a few more minutes.

A prayer that was dashed completely when he heard an enraged bellow echoing down the hallway. "You *bitch*, I'll freaking *kill* you!" A shout underscored by the *CRACK-CRACK-CRACK* of three successive shots.

Chapter Thirteen

Shannon knelt behind the king-size bed, using the plush mattress, with its maroon-and-gold silk comforter, to steady her shaking arms as she took aim at a heavy locked door already perforated by three bullets.

Furious as he was, Red Beard wasn't dumb enough to charge in, nor did he fire any more shots into his boss's bedroom. Instead, she assumed he was lurking outside, listening for any sounds from her while waiting for his backup to arrive.

Meaning she was in big trouble, a realization she reached even before she noticed that the head and foot-boards of the huge bed were equipped with brackets attached to heavy-duty chains and shackles. Bondage restraints meant for willing partners but all too easy for a misogynist like Powers to put to darker use.

Put to use on her, if she allowed herself to be surrounded and taken alive. Deciding she would die before submitting, she reached for the bedside landline and quickly pressed 9-1-1 with the intention of reporting a fire, a bomb or armed intruders—maybe all three—to draw rescuers, and divert Powers's and his men's attention.

Instead of the 9-1-1 dispatcher's voice, Shannon heard nothing but the ringing of the telephone, a reminder of what she'd previously forgotten, that all calls were being routed to Garrett's cell phone. So why wasn't he picking up so she could at least warn him what was happening? Maybe it wasn't too late for him to get a message through to Rafe.

After ten rings his voice mail picked up, and she felt all that was left of her hope ebbing. Had things gone as badly wrong at the hotel as they had here? And what about Rafe? Had he been captured and restrained by Powers's men, or had they killed him on sight instead?

Her mind lurched back to that recklessly impulsive moment when she'd thrown herself into his arms and kissed him before leaving. The strength and the passion and the raw heat she'd felt pouring into her—how could even the blackest evil vanquish such a life force?

Something moved outside the floor-to-ceiling window, a mountain of a bald man with a handgun, edging forward cautiously and clearly looking into the spacious room to try to see her. Freezing in place beside the bed, Shannon scarcely dared to breathe. From this angle, no more than a sliver of her body should be visible, but if he spotted her, one carefully aimed shot could take her out.

Clearly not seeing her, he crept nearer. Then nearer still, until he was reaching for the door she had already tested and found locked.

Apparently he didn't have the key—at least not on him—so he started edging sideways, quickly approaching the perfect angle from which to see Shannon—or shoot her though the glass.

Which left her with a dilemma. Did she try to bolt across the room toward the open doors to the master suite's bath and closet in the hopes of better cover or take her best shot at nailing the man before he—or Red Beard waiting in the hall to come blasting through the door—could kill her?

"Why, oh why, is there never a Door Number Three when a girl needs one?" Shannon murmured just before she made her choice.

RAFE ALMOST RAN HER OVER—a terrified young woman tearing down the hallway with her long black hair flying and a bundle of white blankets in her arms.

Not blankets, he realized, taking in the pink-and-white uniform at the same moment he heard the cries and saw the tiny red face that stopped him in his tracks.

"No, no, *señor*," the woman pleaded. "You mustn't hurt *El Jefe's niño*. He will kill you—kill both of us—if you—"

Rafe grabbed the baby in an instant, shifting the bundle to one arm and tucking it against his body like a football. "That's damned well *not* your boss's baby, and you know it. Is she the only one? Where are all the others?"

Her black eyes bulging, she shuddered visibly. "I—I cannot—"

Rafe speared her with a hard look that had her stammering, "N-no—no others right now. This the only one left. But Señor Powers, he will kill—"

"We'll see who does the killing. Now tell me, what's going on here? And have you seen another woman, a young housekeeper you didn't recognize?"

The nursemaid shook her head. "I clean up in the baby room. Nobody else come in there unless *El Jefe* bring them."

"What about his ledger?" he asked; then, noticing

her confused look, he clarified. "It's a book he writes in, one with leather binding."

She opened her mouth to answer, then snapped it shut at the sound of fast-approaching footsteps from the direction Rafe had just come. At nearly the same instant they heard shots from the opposite direction, followed by some heavy cracking sounds, as if something were striking against a door or wall.

With a squeak of terror, the young woman took a few steps before opening an interior door and rushing through it. With the baby in his arms—a tiny, blue-eyed infant Rafe instinctively believed was his own niece—drawing attention with her crying, he forced his way inside behind her, then closed and locked the door.

Scanning the windowless room, he saw something he had not expected, much less allowed himself to hope for—a sterile, hospital-style nursery with four tiny bassinets and what he thought might be an incubator. As the young woman had claimed, all were empty. While she ran shrieking to lock herself inside a small bathroom, Rafe laid the baby in a bassinet and aimed his weapon at the door, determined to guard it with his life before allowing armed men to breach the entry.

Instead, he heard them rush past, shouting to someone ahead of them. Relieved not to have a shootout erupting with the helpless infant so close, he turned to glance at where the impossibly small baby kicked her chubby arms and legs and wailed, filling his heart with a single, undeniable imperative.

Getting her out of here right now, before little Amber Lee became the tiniest casualty in what was quickly turning out to be a bloodbath.

But that meant abandoning Shannon to her fate, if she

was, as he suspected, at the heart of the disturbance. If she was still alive, after those last shots he had heard.

At the thought, his mouth went bone-dry, a fresh jolt of adrenaline charging through his system. As a Ranger, it went against his code to ever leave a team member behind, regardless of the circumstance. And as a man, it went against his very nature to turn his back on any woman—but especially a woman for whom he felt such...

No. He couldn't allow emotions or anything else to keep him from fulfilling the promise he had made to Garrett. The last vow he had made to his murdered sister—a younger sister he had loved and raised, only to send out into a cruel world—from beside her coffin as it was swallowed by the devouring earth.

Taking the baby back into his arms, he rocked her awkwardly and whispered, "It's all right. It's gonna be okay, sweetheart. Uncle Rafe is getting you out of here right now." *Even if I have to blast our way through an army to get you to safety.*

Moments later he was running with his niece back through the house, every step he took tearing at his soul. Groping desperately for some alternative, he thought of stashing Amber somewhere in the villa or the van until he could help Shannon, then go back for her. But what if he were cut off from the spot or outright killed? What if he were risking his niece for a woman who was lost already?

Forced to make the gut-wrenching choice to leave Shannon for the infant's safety, he somehow managed to get out without encountering any more guards. Securing the baby as best he could in the middle seat of the van, he drove up to the gate unchallenged, then slowly forced it open and drove the van through.

Under other circumstances he might have whooped with joy as they reached the street with no pursuit in sight. After all, he had succeeded, had managed, despite the longest of odds, to reclaim his sister's stolen baby and get out with both their lives.

Yet rather than victory or elation, the Ranger known to his men as the Lion drove away in silence. A silence broken only by the crying infant behind his back, who kicked away the folds of a white blanket to reveal the soft blue cotton outfit underneath.

Chapter Fourteen

The spreading shot from Shannon's first blast took out the huge window, which dropped in a curtain of lethal shards that shattered against the lower frame and floor. Seizing on the crash her opponent couldn't have expected, she took a running leap through the newly made opening, firing a second, then a third, round to pepper the stunned man with lead as he raised his gun toward her.

Though she would have preferred the stopping power of traditional bullets, the scatter from the Taurus's shotgun shells compensated for her running aim, and the shock of pain had the guard retreating, even while squeezing off several desperation shots that went wild.

Shrieking a battle cry that she hoped might further unnerve him, Shannon was almost on the huge man by the time he took aim at her. She pulled her trigger first, the revolver barking and the shot biting as it caught his neck and shoulder.

He avalanched to the ground, streamers of blood spouting from a severed artery and his fingers squeezing reflexively to fire one last shot. Shannon felt it before she heard it—a white-hot slash of pain that she was far too busy running to stop and analyze.

Sprinting toward the ocean that could prove either her salvation or her deathbed.

RAFE CRUISED ALONG South Ocean Boulevard, slowing for the traffic as he threaded his way through the surfers, wannabes and gawkers gathering for their daily worship of the cresting blue swells. Plenty of skin was on display, some toned and bronzed and youthful, some leathery and crinkled from too many endless summers beneath the tropical sun.

Should he be looking for a payphone where he could anonymously report on shots fired at the mansion? Or would doing so alarm Powers to the point that he would permanently silence Shannon if he had her?

Deciding against the call for now, Rafe pulled into one of the few parking spaces, then he jumped out of the van just long enough to strip off the magnetized sign before climbing back inside to change into a dark blue T-shirt. As he did, he looked down anxiously at the baby, who had stopped crying and fallen asleep along the way.

Was that a normal thing, or was something wrong? Rafe might be able to field strip, clean and reassemble a firearm in next to no time, but when it came to something as tiny and fragile as a newborn, he barely knew one end from the other. Except that one was always getting wet, the other hungry, and he had no way to deal with either pressing need. He would need some sort of car seat, too, while he was at it. Why hadn't he and Garrett seriously thought about the possibility the baby might still be in Powers's villa?

Frowning at the thought of Garrett, Rafe reached down to rearrange the blanket and carefully, almost tentatively, stroke the powder-soft flesh of the plump leg. "Don't you worry, sweetie. We'll find out about your daddy, and we'll get you taken care of—and pick you out a couple of pretty new girls' things while we're at it."

Because even Rafe knew it was like some kind of law, you didn't go dressing a baby girl in blue. You didn't...

"Oh, *hell!*" he said, his head shaking and his hand jerking away as if he'd been stung. "Tell me I didn't— That you aren't really—"

Heart jackhammering in his chest, he told himself that the idiots in the mansion had dressed Amber Lee—it *had* to be his sister's baby—in what they'd had on hand, that was all. That the connection he had felt when he'd first peered down into those blue eyes had been pure instinct, not a mistake.

That he hadn't abandoned the woman he had grown to care for to her fate to save a stranger's child.

Biting back the impulse to swear, he decided he couldn't take knowing for sure, not yet. Scrambling into the front seat to escape, he put the van in gear with the intention of driving to a drug or discount or grocery store—anywhere he might pick up the things he needed.

He didn't get six inches before he braked and drove back into his spot, waving an apology at the driver whose surfboard-bearing SUV was waiting for him to leave. Barely noticing when the surfers flipped him off, Rafe put the van back into Park and once more squeezed between the front seats.

"I don't know if Shannon's alive or suffering or dead in that house," he told the sleeping innocent as tears burned in his eyes. "Don't know whether your dad— whether Garrett's—been hurt or killed or taken into custody. So you're gonna have to excuse this intrusion, kiddo. Because this might be the one thing, the only thing I can be sure of right now, and I can't stand another second of not knowing."

The words faded as he made adjustments, working so carefully, he might have been defusing a deadly bomb. His suddenly oversize fingers slid down the tiny blue diaper cover, pulling loose first one tab, then the second. Finally he whispered, "Here goes nothing, Amber," as he pulled the front of the diaper open.

And whether it was in response to the sound of his voice, the cool air from the van's AC, or Rafe's use of the name, the baby slitted open blue eyes and chose that moment to offer up a shining stream of evidence that he was certainly no girl.

MADISON WAS THROWING UP AGAIN, Everett realized, listening at the bathroom door she had locked so he wouldn't try to stop her. He'd suspected it for a few weeks now, since he had triumphantly—and idiotically, he now realized—brought home the baby he had hoped would finally kick her out of her funk and turn her back into the happy twenty-three-year-old he loved to spoil.

Instead she seemed more stressed than ever, the weight falling off her and her obsession with that idiot dog Suki's videos and photo albums growing by the day. As for the baby he'd spent a king's ransom to get in a "specially expedited" adoption, the little girl he had named Zinnia, since his agent had assured him that offbeat flower names were all the rage now, Maddi had barely looked at her, had said to call the kid whatever he wanted and still referred to her as "it."

She had perked up just a little when he'd shared the adoption attorney's assurances that the babies he placed were the cream of the crop, infants quietly surrendered by the best sorts of young women who didn't want their Ivy League educations interrupted by an unplanned pregnancy. He had been especially excited at the thought of—and paid a hefty premium for—a girl who matched his young third wife's fair skin and dark hair, and whose birth mother had been green-eyed.

Zinnia's eyes, he had noticed the last time he'd stopped in to see her in the nursery, were still stubbornly blue, but when he'd called to complain, Powers had told him it could take up to a year for their true color to become apparent. Everett had rather been hoping the attorney might offer an exchange or refund, but Powers had instead assured him of how incredibly fortunate he'd been to receive such a high-caliber newborn in the first place.

Fortunate indeed, thought Everett, as he stood beside the door and listened to his young wife's retching. If he had it to do over, he would have saved his money—or quit listening to his publicist and sent Maddi back into inpatient treatment where she belonged.

BEYOND A CERTAIN POINT, not even adrenaline can propel the human body. Struggling for one more stroke, one effective kick against the current, Shannon felt the spasms of exhaustion grip her, limb by leaden limb.

Coordination lost, she floundered, and the warm Atlantic, as if waiting for its opening, closed over her head.

I'm sorry, Dad. Sorry I turned out to be such a disappointment. But it was not her father whose image filled her mind and made her fight her way back to the surface to suck in one more breath.

It was the example of Rafe's determination, the

sacrifice he was making for his family and the memory of his arms around her that lifted her up. Toward the air and toward the brilliant white light...

A white light that turned out to be the sun's.

"Miss, miss. You're okay now. You're on shore—open your eyes."

She blinked, taking in the bony man who knelt above her. Wearing a red ball cap and wet nylon shorts with soaked running shoes, he tried without much success to prevent a dripping golden retriever from crowding in and licking her face.

"What? What happened?" she asked, pushing away the dog's warm kisses. *How on earth am I alive?*

"I was running with Lucky here when he started going crazy barking, plunging into the surf. I ran to drag him back out, and that's when I saw you struggling. The two of us together pulled you out."

"Thank you!" Groaning as she sat up, Shannon hugged the retriever's neck, then clasped the runner's thin but strong arm. "Thank you both so much. You're a couple of lifesavers. Good dog, Lucky."

The golden wagged and kissed her as she stroked his ears.

"Maybe you should lie down. I'll flag down somebody to call an ambulance. Would do it myself, but my phone was in my pocket—and it's not waterproof."

She struggled to her feet, shaking her head. "Sorry about your phone, but please don't bother. I'm okay now. I promise."

Looking down the beach, she saw a row of mansions, including Powers's villa, not nearly far enough away. If his men found her here, they would no doubt kill her—perhaps taking out any witnesses, as well. Including her rescuers.

"Do you work nearby?" the man asked, his hazel eyes studying her sodden uniform. "Can I walk you somewhere?"

"I, uh, live near here," she said, staggering toward the sidewalk. "It's not far, and I have clothes there."

"Please, miss, that's blood on you, isn't it?" He reached toward her. "You shouldn't—"

"Please, no. I'm fine."

"If you're sure that's what you want." Reluctantly, he turned from her, looking hurt and angry. "C'mon, Lucky. Let's go, boy."

Without another word, he and the dog bounded away, leaving Shannon to stagger off the beach.

She wasn't sure whether she wandered the streets for twenty minutes or six hours, with sand clinging to the uniform and her hair in stiffening clumps. Like the gun, her shoes were long gone, and the bottoms of her feet were blistering on the hot pavement. That pain blended with the others, so many she couldn't stop to catalog them.

No cars slowed as they passed her; no one called out for her to stop. Perhaps they thought she was intoxicated, a homeless woman or a victim of some domestic situation they didn't care to get involved with. Whatever the case, no one came out of the big houses or the small businesses that sprang up farther from the beach, and the people she passed failed to make eye contact.

Shannon couldn't blame them. She had checked out of her own mind and was simply wandering in shock, exhausted, unable to form a single coherent thought, let alone any idea of what she should do next. As the tropical heat built, her fog persisted, short-circuiting even her sense of self-preservation when a vehicle stopped beside her and a large man pulled her inside.

Chapter Fifteen

August 26

Awareness began with a single touch, with the sensation of fingers sliding through her tangled hair and cradling the back of her head.

"Shannon, drink this. Please drink. We can't have you getting dehydrated again."

Still only half-conscious, she did as she was asked when he held a water bottle to her lips, responding instinctively to a male voice she knew and trusted, though she could not yet place it. She managed a sip before her body suddenly remembered it was starved for water, leaving her to choke and sputter as she gulped too much at once and fell back against something soft.

Pulling her upright, he gently thumped her back. "Whoa, there. Take it easy, sugar."

Rafe. Her eyes fluttered open, and she fought to focus. To make sure this was no dream.

"Hey there, cowboy," she said in a voice like the hiss of blown sand against a window.

He smiled down at her, his gaze shadowed with fatigue and worry. And then the smile withered as some deeper emotion shone in his green eyes.

"Don't ever do that again." Pointing at her, he shifted

uncomfortably in a straight-backed chair that seemed too delicate to support two hundred pounds of lean muscle and raw determination. "Don't ever scare me like that—promise."

"Scare you?" What on earth had she done?

"By the time I found you yesterday, I was already half-convinced I'd lost you. Then, when I looked into your eyes and realized you weren't looking back..." In his strong jaw, a muscle spasmed. "I realized those sons of bitches might not have left enough of you *to* come back."

"I was... I was lost," she whispered, remembering the pain radiating through her, the heat waves rising from the pavement, the imperative to keep moving, but almost nothing else.

"Lost and beat to hell, from the looks of you. Slashed along your side, too. Doc thinks you might've had a very close call with a bullet. Do you remember?"

Gaze drifting, she thought back to the villa, and the horror of it came back to her in bits and pieces, memories as sharp as mirrored shards. Finally she nodded. "Yeah, I think so. Most of it, anyway."

He shook his head, regret shining in his eyes. "I'm sorry, Shannon, sorrier than you can ever imagine that you ended up hurt. Before I grabbed you, I thought I could live with risking your life, with coercing you into helping with this crazy—"

"I was in it," she said, pain arcing from her back to her side as she twisted to grab the water bottle, "because I *chose* to be. You know that."

"I left you there." Rafe's face was a mask of misery. "Left you because I couldn't—"

"It doesn't matter," she said, trusting that this man, this war hero, had done everything he could.

"It damned well matters to *me*," he insisted. "I should've found some way. I should have—"

"Let me have a little more." She tried to lift the bottle.

He helped her take a few more sips, his hands supporting her. "Slowly this time, or you'll get sick.... That's enough for right now."

Setting the water on a white wicker nightstand, he laid her gently among soft pillows, giving her a chance to take in the soft green walls, white wicker dresser and cheery tropical comforter. She noticed photos on the wall, framed pictures of a handsome family clowning on the beach, goofing off in a theme park or showing off their strings of fresh-caught fish.

"This isn't a hotel," she decided. "This is someone's house, right?"

"It's a friend's vacation condo. Doc's a combat medic. He's the one who checked you out and hydrated you with an IV," Rafe explained, still looking regretful. "Gave you something for the pain, too, but I don't suppose you remember any of that. You were pretty out of it."

She shook her head in answer, wondering if these men helping Rafe ever stopped to think about what they were risking. "So where's Garrett? And what—what happened at the villa?"

Fresh pain darkened Rafe's eyes, and he looked toward the window, its shade drawn like the corners of his mouth—that sensuous mouth she remembered kissing so recklessly.

"What is it?" Worry had her stomach knotting. "What's going on?"

"Let's get you taken care of first. Do you want to try to eat, or do you need to use the bathroom?"

Ignoring the suggestion, she reached out to grab

his hand and gave it a squeeze. "Tell me, Rafe. Please tell me."

He nodded, the line of his mouth grim.

"Something happened back at the hotel after I left for the villa." He had to clear his throat before resuming, his hand pulling free of her grip to curl into a hard fist. "I was on the phone with Garrett when I heard pounding. And what sounded like the door being kicked in."

"What?" Alarm goosed her heart rate. "Who kicked it in? Was he taken into custody?"

The breath froze in her lungs as she pictured the members of her task force grilling him, demanding to know what had happened to her. They would have found clothing and other items Rafe had purchased for her in the room. Would certainly by now be realizing that she was a willing conspirator rather than dead or the victim of an abduction.

"That's what I'm hoping," Rafe said. "As tough a break as that would be, at least he'd be safe with the authorities. Alive."

"You don't know?"

His eyes shuttered, and he shook his head, his hands gripping his own tensed thighs.

Shannon pushed herself to a sitting position, ignoring the pain of her injuries and waiting out the dizziness that washed over her at the change in elevation. In place of the filthy housekeeper's uniform, she realized, someone had dressed her in a soft peach nightshirt, vastly oversize but clean. Trying not to think of Rafe, perhaps with his friend, removing her ruined clothing, she reached out to stroke the Ranger's arm, her fingertips trailing along the corded muscle, bumping over the thickened line of an old scar.

"You're worried it was another attack, aren't you? Like that night at the motel?" she asked.

Rafe nodded. "I have someone checking on it, but I'm definitely concerned that's what happened. That whoever it was broke in and shot him on the spot."

If it were true, it would be so unfair—the final insult to a man who had already had so much taken from him so cruelly. Flawed as he was, Garrett had risked everything to reclaim what might remain of his family, had worked tirelessly alongside Rafe to make it happen. "There was nothing on the news?"

"No. Which makes me wonder whether the authorities are keeping a lid on the story for some reason. They're probably hoping I'll come back."

"Or that *I* will," Shannon added, hating to imagine the interrogation she had coming, though her colleagues would start gently, calling it a "debriefing" to begin with. Feigning sensitivity, they would gradually attempt to lure her into making self-incriminating statements. Unless she returned with Rafe in custody.

"But what if it was Powers?" Rafe asked. "If it's been him all along? Could be he's onto what we're up to and has taken out Garrett as a warning, or maybe captured him to use as a hostage."

"Poor Garrett," she murmured.

Rafe nodded, his eyes grim. "Whatever's happened to him, he's beyond our help for the time being. We need to focus now on Powers and the babies."

But Shannon was still stuck on the thought of Powers's ice-cold voice, the cruelty he seemed to relish. Nausea swirled inside her at the thought of what means he might employ to extract information from a man who had already suffered so much as a result of the attorney's bottomless greed.

But that wasn't right, she realized, shaking her head. "I spoke to Powers at the villa, and I can tell you, he didn't have a clue what we're up to."

"Then he hasn't guessed there's any connection to my sister?"

"He was furious at catching me bursting out of his office only seconds before the outage, believe me, but he didn't seem to—"

"He's the one who did this to you?" Rafe's voice dropped to a low growl, his eyes narrowing dangerously.

"What I'm getting at," she said, determined not to be sidetracked, "is that Powers acted shocked, almost bewildered, to find an intruder. Maybe he spends so much time conning prospective adopters, he's conned himself, too, and thinks his money and his brains have made him untouchable. He was certainly thrown off when I lied and told him I was spying for the IRS, out for some reward for turning in a tax cheat."

"So if he really didn't know about us," Rafe said, "that means we were right before. He really didn't send the guys who shot up our motel room and threw the Molotov cocktail."

"So who did?" Shannon asked him. "Because whoever it was, that could be who nabbed Garrett."

Rafe stood and started pacing. "You know what? I think it's that game—that damned game Garrett was wrapped up in. What if one of his hacker buddies figured out a way to track him by using his logins to the 'Battle Bloodcraft' system?"

"How would they manage that?"

Rafe raked his fingers through his black hair, his green eyes shining like a panther's. "I'm no computer expert, but what if they found a way to go through the game server to pass along some sort of virus that would report his coordinates even after he stopped logging on?"

She nodded. "I told you, some of these pals of his were serious outlaws—serious enough to orchestrate a cyber-attack that nearly took over U.S. missile silos."

Rafe gave a low whistle. "You think they meant to launch our nukes?"

"Or hold them hostage, or just embarrass the government for kicks. Whatever their intentions, they're dangerous as all hell. But why would they be coming after Garrett?"

"I'd like to think he was smart enough not to mention that we were carrying a lot of cash," Rafe said, "but heaven knows, his judgment could've been off, considering the state he's been in these past few weeks."

"You really think these hackers might have been tracking us to steal your money?"

"Cash, weapons, whatever they could grab."

She shook her head. "No offense to your nest egg, Rafe, but these guys could pull down a lot bigger scores than your savings and a few weapons, and with far less personal risk, just by using the 'net to rip off people's bank accounts."

"Maybe the risk is the whole point," Rafe said. "Maybe these wannabe commandos are playing out their fantasies in real life."

"Yeah, I can see that," she said, thinking of the sloppiness of the initial raid. "Could be that a couple of his hacker friends let their addiction to the game trump whatever sympathy they felt for Garrett's loss."

"If those losers had the capacity to ever really feel human emotion in the first place." Rafe bowed his head, rubbing at his temples, as if that might erase his stress and exhaustion. "That's what this all boils down to. People—from those hackers to Dominic Powers—without a shred of compassion for anyone else, not even for an innocent young woman living for the day she could hold her first baby in her arms. Now she'll never have that, and her kid will never have the chance to know who she was."

Fighting past the pain in her lower back, her ribs and what felt like a thousand lesser injuries, Shannon rose from the bed. Knees wobbling with the effort, she took her first step.

Rafe crossed the room in an instant and grabbed her elbow to support her. "Careful there. Where're you heading so fast?"

"Right here," she said softly as she wrapped her arms around his ribs and hugged him tightly. "I was heading right here, Rafe, to tell you how sorry I am about Lissa—and Garrett, whatever's happened to him. So sorry that so many things have gone wrong."

For a while they said nothing, his strong hands stroking her back as their bodies comforted each other in a slow, rocking embrace. Though the August heat outside was sultry and his chest so warm against her cheek, Shannon was catapulted back in time, feeling the cool breath of snowcapped mountains, hearing the creak of saddle leather. For a moment confusion spiraled through her—why the déjà vu? Why now, carrying her back to her beloved Montana?

His warm lips brushed her temple, an answering caress. Rafe might not hail from Montana, but some part of her recognized the arms of this Ranger, who had started his life as a rough-and-tumble cowboy, as the true home she'd been seeking for the greater part of her life.

Her knees loosened with the thought, with the knowledge that though they had never shared—must never share—a bed, her sympathies had already gone well past the point of no return with this man. A man who had thrown away his future for what now seemed a hopeless quest.

As her heart sagged, Rafe helped her back to the bed. "You're still weak, sugar. Are you hurting?"

She shook her head. "That's not important right now. I have to tell you everything that happened. Have to tell you what I learned in Powers's villa."

"Not until you've eaten and had the chance to clean up. I've brought more clothes for you, too. And you really should take something. Anybody could see you're in pain."

Though she argued, Rafe insisted, and she realized he was right. She had to take care of her body first, to tend her wounds and needs, or she wouldn't be fit to make decisions about what came next.

Declining the offer of something stronger, she accepted two aspirin. Rafe went to the kitchen and returned a few minutes later carrying a warmed plate of what looked like homemade macaroni and cheese with sliced ham, and a small cup of fruit. Comfort food, she thought, touched by the unexpected effort.

"I *could* tell you I made it myself," he said with a disarming grin, "but I wouldn't want you to go into shock later, when you have to eat my real cooking."

"Let me guess, it's all Manwiches and barbecue for you," she laughed, "washed down with a six-pack of something brewed in Texas."

"Don't knock it 'til you've tried it." But his grin quickly faltered, the light winking out in his eyes as if it was only now hitting him that there would never be an occasion for her to find out about his cooking. That these fleeting, desperate moments were all the two of them would ever have.

You can't do this. Can't afford to read so much into a look, a hug, a single quick kiss. But no matter how much Shannon warned herself against her feelings, the hollow ache continued to build up inside her. An ache that warned her of the pain in store if she let this go any further.

"You go ahead and eat," Rafe said, already turning from her. "Let me know as soon as you're done, and I'll help you to the bathroom."

"Thanks, Rafe."

He shook his head and murmured, "Least I could do after getting you into this." With one last, pained look, he slipped out of the room.

Though she knew she should be hungry, Shannon barely managed a third of the meal before giving up in frustration. Pushing herself up from the bed, she used the nightstand to steady herself before heading for the door. From somewhere down the hallway, she heard Rafe speaking—to someone on the phone, she thought. Probably to one of the Rangers helping him.

Determined not to interrupt, she made it to the sparkling small bathroom, where he had thoughtfully left a few toiletries, along with a folded pile of clothing whose silky feel told her that he'd gone somewhere nicer than the discount store she might have expected. Closing the door, she carefully peeled off the nightshirt before risking her first look at her injuries.

At the sight of the huge purple bruise along her rib cage, she sucked in a breath through her clenched teeth, her mind catapulted back to the beating Red Beard had inflicted at his boss's direction. Several inches lower, on the same side, an adhesive bandage covered what she supposed must be the graze wound Rafe had mentioned. Relying on the mirror, she found even deeper bruising on her lower back, a sight that had her eyes watering with the memory of the blows she'd taken, punches she was not surprised to find, once she finally managed to sit down, left her urine tinted pink.

Telling herself she would already be dead if the injury were serious, she turned on the shower and tried to scrub away the memory of the ugly threats, the terror, the arterial blood spraying from the neck wound she'd inflicted on the guard who would have killed her. Though she'd had no choice about killing him, she would certainly be called on to explain the reason she had gone to the villa in the first place.

Facing her family would be even harder than talking to her supervisors. Would her brother and her uncle turn their backs on her forever for tainting the proud Brandt legacy with disgrace? Could anyone she knew begin to understand? How could they, when she couldn't even justify her choices in her own mind?

By the time she turned off the water, she was trembling with exhaustion, her eyes leaking tears that had finally burned their way through her defenses. With the towel wound around her torso, she managed to brush her teeth before trying—and failing—to comb the tangles from her wet hair, a failure that only had her crying harder.

Just like a damned girl, she thought, recalling her bachelor uncle's stinging words, his scornful look before he had turned his face from her weakness in the months after her father's murder. Four years older, her brother had been quicker to adapt, to conform to their rancher uncle's version of the masculine ideal. In her desperate bid for the old man's love, she'd turned tomboy in a hurry, locked her tears away where they could no longer hurt her.

Not that it had done a thing to reform Uncle Lloyd's opinion of her. Nothing had, until the day she announced her intention to follow in her father's footsteps. Even then, it was understood that the old man never really expected her to make the bureau, that he had pinned all his hope and pride on Steve, his chosen heir.

There was a soft tap at the door before Rafe asked, "You all right in there?"

"Su-sure," she said, but her broken answer had him cracking the door open.

"Let me help you. Let me…"

Helpless against the tears she had bottled up for so long, she made a sound, a quiet sniffle, that gave her away.

He came inside and carefully scooped her into his arms before carrying her back into the bedroom. As he laid her back atop the sheets, she whispered, "Sorry, Rafe. I'm sorry."

"For what?" he asked, his fingertips brushing her knee, only an inch or so from the border of yet another bruise.

"For being so much trouble. For being such a girl."

This time, when he sat, it was on the bed's edge rather than the chair. Once more he enveloped her in his arms, not complaining when she rested her damp head against his shoulder.

"A woman," he corrected. "One hell of a woman, and I've gotta tell you, Shannon, I'm awfully glad you are. Because if you were a guy, I'd be pretty worried right now, the way I've been thinking about you. The way I've been feeling."

She blew out a long breath, relaxing into the gentleness of his embrace. Could it really be true that he didn't mind her weakness? That a battle-hardened Ranger didn't hold her tears in contempt?

"Be right back," he said. After leaving for a minute, he returned with her clothes and several other items, including a dry towel, which he laid across her shoulders.

Next he combed out her hair, his movements slow and deft as he untangled the snarls.

Her gaze flicked to his green eyes, admiring their quiet focus. She couldn't remember the last time anyone had combed her hair so carefully. "They teach you this on the rodeo circuit?"

"Oh, I've brushed out my share of knotted horse tails." He grinned and winked before admitting, "Really, I earned my stripes tending to Lissa. My mom went back to work, and I was the one elected to get Lissa up and ready for the kindergarten bus. I complained, of course, but I miss it. I miss all of them—our folks died in a wreck ten years back."

"That's rough. I lost my folks young, too. I can barely remember what Mom looked like. My dad was pretty great, though, at least until he…"

"I'm sorry," Rafe said, reminding her how he had known about her father's murder. How he had thrown it up in her face after grabbing her off the street.

But they'd been enemies then, neither reluctant allies nor friends. If friendship formed any part of the swirling emotion she felt as he dried her hair with tender care.

"There," he said, once he was finished, his fingertips caressing silky strands and his eyes searching hers as he added, "That feels… It feels better, doesn't it? Feels so…"

She looked back at him in answer. Looked back into

the face of a man she dared not claim but ached to kiss. *One more taste. Just one more.*

Unable to stop herself, she leaned in, breathing his name before gently, tentatively, touching her lips to his. And feeling, only moments later, humiliation sear her face when he firmly grasped her shoulders and told her, "This isn't right."

Chapter Sixteen

Rafe saw fresh pain bloom in her eyes, pain that he'd inflicted this time. And he ached to erase it, to kiss away her hurt and make her forget the beating she had taken.

Hell, who was he kidding? He wanted to forget, too, to lose himself in raw sex. In *her*. To lift the floodgates of a passion so destructive it would wash everything else away.

He wanted Shannon Brandt beneath him, but he couldn't even think of it without guilt roaring through him at what she'd suffered on his behalf. What he hadn't so far been able to bear knowing she might have suffered.

But it was time to man up now, to find out, no matter what it cost him. "I have to ask you something about Powers and his men. And I need you to be honest, no matter how tough it might be."

Blush fading, she shook her head. "What do you mean? I don't understand."

"Shannon, did he—did he rape you? Did that animal... Did any of them...?" His words choked down to an anguished standstill.

"Oh, no, Rafe. No," she told him, tears standing in her blue eyes. "There were threats, horrible threats, and I have no doubt at all that sadist has it in him. But I threw him off with lies, and then I shot my way out."

She was trembling as she spoke, and he took her into his arms, rocking her and kissing her crown softly. Except that this time, when she looked up at him, he covered her mouth with his, the immensity of his relief mixing with a need he'd suppressed for so long that it rose from his chest in a rumble deeper and more powerful than a lion's growl.

Her lips parted to his questing tongue, her answering moan stoking the hot flare of his passion, and before he knew what happened they were embracing on the bed together, on a bed where anything and everything could happen. But in spite of the animal imperative of his lust, he fought to pull back from it, to remind himself of his true mission. When that didn't work, he dug deeper, calling back the fear he'd felt when he'd looked into her hollow eyes—fear that had turned to shock when he'd seen the lurid bruising that marred her smooth flesh.

Pulling away, he opened his mouth, intent on saying something sensible. She silenced him by fumbling to release the towel wrapped damp and tight around her chest, her gaze misty with desire.

The towel fell open, and she lay back amid the tumbled sheets, watching as he watched her, his gaze feasting on the sight of her nude body, on the invitation in her jewel-bright eyes.

One hand hovering only an inch or two above her breast, he forced himself to focus on the dark edge of a bruise. Groaning with frustration, he forced his hand to drop away. "I can't, Shannon. Much as I want to—and right now, I'd just about sell my soul to have you." He struggled to shake off the building ache. "But you're hurt, and I couldn't live with causing you more pain."

"You'd never hurt me," she whispered, her eyes swallowing him whole. "I trust you. And I want you. Need to feel your skin against mine. Please, just…make me forget. Make both of us forget…for just a little while."

Grasping his hand, she pushed it to her breast, and that quickly, he was lost in the warmth of silken skin, the soft roundness that peaked into a hardened nipple. Forgetting his other obligations, he lay down beside her, testing the fullness of each firm breast and running his palms over her body without ever allowing his weight to fall upon her.

She arched her neck, exposing it for him to feast on the pale flesh, to flick his tongue into her ear and revel in her moan of pleasure—a sound that sent a bolt of pure need blazing through his body. Still he blocked her efforts to unbutton his shirt, ignored her invitations for him to undress, too, though by now his pants were so tight, he wanted nothing more than to free his straining erection.

Instead he moved slowly, carefully, suckling each perfect breast in turn, then kissing his way down to her flat stomach to lave her navel with his tongue while exploring the hot, wet core of her with eager fingers. When she gasped, he looked anxiously toward her face. "Are you all right? Am I hurting you?"

"No, don't stop. Please…" she pleaded.

Ranger school had been tough, Afghanistan and his other missions even harder. But walling off his own need, his body's drive to take her, demanded every ounce of determination he'd learned on the field of battle. Burying his head between her legs, he tasted what he could not have, stroking her slowly, tentatively at first, then faster, following her lead until every muscle in her body tightened and then released in a climax that tore his name from her mouth....

On the heels of her cry came another, a whimpering that built to a demand—the baby crying from the family room where Rafe had left him fast asleep.

UNDONE BY PLEASURE, by Rafe's tenderness and care, Shannon didn't hear at first—probably wouldn't have heard a SWAT team blasting its way through the front door. Instead, she was reaching toward him, saying, "You now, Rafe. Please let me," when the noise registered, a wailing that sounded almost like...

"What *is* that?" She sat up sharply, grunting at her reawakening pain.

Rafe, too, had reacted, jerking to his feet, guilt flashing in his green eyes. "Sorry, Shannon. I never should have— We can't— Let me take care of this. I'll be right back."

"Take care of *what?*" she asked, her need for him doused in an icy wave of confusion.

But she was speaking to a closed door, because Rafe had left the room already, leaving her scrambling to understand what was happening. After choosing a soft white T-shirt and blue pants, she dressed as quickly as her injuries allowed.

Doubt slowed her even more than pain—doubt that the man who wouldn't even take off his clothes felt any more for her than pity. For as tender as he'd been with her, Rafe hadn't forgotten his true focus for a moment.

So how was it that she'd forgotten hers? Forgotten herself in a moment of weakness she was already regretting, knowing nothing good could come of this. Nothing real or permanent, no matter how right it felt.

Heading for the door, she vowed to follow Rafe's lead—and even more, to pretend that this had never happened and get her mind back on her own mission: bringing in the man whose touch had rocked her to her core.

As Rafe walked out to the small living area dominated by a futon and chairs covered in bright fabrics, he couldn't believe he'd lost control with Shannon. With Garrett and Lissa's baby still among the missing and his plan in flames, he had started down a path he had no right to set foot on.

Worse yet, he had further compromised Shannon, risking her again when he had sworn—had been swearing since the moment he had found her on the street so damaged—that if she survived her ordeal, he was cutting her loose from this.

"Hey, little guy, I'm right here." Bypassing the muted TV, which was displaying the local weather forecast, Rafe bent down to unlatch the carrier where he'd left the infant sleeping beside the coffee table. Apparently naptime was over, because the baby kicked his feet and waved his tiny arms, his face reddening as his cries intensified.

Barely glancing at the television's graphic, which read *Tropical Weather Update,* Rafe changed the wet diaper. The crying went on, so he picked up the infant, supporting the fuzzy head as he walked the baby boy around the room. "You know, it'd be a heck of a lot easier if you'd let me know what you want."

Smacking his lips, the baby nuzzled Rafe's chest and rooted around as if he meant to— "What the heck, dude?" Rafe asked, then broke out laughing as he realized the attempt at nursing was the little guy's way of giving Rafe the information he'd requested.

"What's so funny?" When he turned toward the sound of Shannon's voice, Rafe saw her staring at him as if he'd grown an extra head. Fortunately she had dressed. Not that the baby would care, but Rafe had already established that her naked body was enough to derail his best intentions.

"You—you *found* her?" Shannon's words tumbled free, picking up speed with her excitement. "Rafe, why didn't you tell me you'd found Lissa's baby? Paloma let something slip about little ones being in the villa. That's what I was trying to tell you earlier. But this—this is wonderful. She's gorgeous. Perfect. Won't Garrett be so—"

Rafe grimaced. "This isn't Garrett's daughter. It isn't Amber Lee. I thought so, too, when I got us out of that place, but then I found out… It was a real shock, I'll admit it. But we're working to find this little fellow's family. To make this one thing right, or at least as right as it can be made."

The tiny fists and feet stirred, and the baby's cherub's lips moved. Shannon drifted toward them, the yearning in her face so clear that Rafe read her desire to pick up the newborn, to reassure herself that at least one lost child was whole and healthy.

"What about the others?" she asked.

"I checked the nursery, but he was the only one there. Which means someone must already have adopted Lissa's baby. And I *will* find out what Powers did with her, with all of them. I'll find them if it's the last thing I do."

"Rafe? Did you ever stop to think, to prepare yourself in case… Considering the circumstances of their births, the blood loss and the trauma, it's likely that not all those babies made it."

"Lissa's baby would have," Rafe insisted, his heart pounding. "My sister was young and strong and healthy."

Their eyes met, the connection between them flaring despite his attempts to quash it. *Please, Shannon, don't say any more about it.*

"I'm going to find my niece alive and thriving. I'm going to take Amber to her father and put her in Garrett's arms where she belongs."

"I'm praying that you will," Shannon told him. "That *we* will."

"Not you," he murmured, rocking the baby as he once more began fussing. "You're heading home, where you'll be safe."

"Not without you, I'm not."

Their gazes clashed, and in hers he saw a question. Would he try to use what had passed between them to weaken her resolve to bring him in? Turning from her, Rafe tried to soothe the baby, his big hands feeling clumsy as he stroked the tiny back.

Shannon seized on the chance to change the subject, an awkward smile tilting lips still swollen from his kisses. "You're really into it, aren't you? Taking care of him?"

"Has to be done." Rafe shrugged, though he admitted to himself, at least, that it was a heck of a kick, holding something so tiny, so helpless, yet so full of potential. It made him wonder how it would feel being a real father, watching his own kid grow, building his own family. Not that he would ever be in a position to find out.

"I'm— It's time to make his bottle," he said. "Do you want to hold him?"

"Sure. Okay." Though she tried not to look too eager,

Rafe noticed how quick Shannon was to take the tiny boy and how natural she looked, laying the infant against her shoulder, walking him and shushing him with quiet tones.

"You look like a real pro," Rafe commented as he walked into the kitchen.

As he looked at her over the counter dividing the two rooms, her smile was soft, her blue eyes wistful. He wondered if she had the slightest idea how appealing she was, how very beautiful.

"My friend Christine has twin boys," she explained. "They're a real handful, but sometimes..."

Though Shannon said no more, he felt her unspoken longing, the path her career, her pursuit of her father's legacy, had left no room for.

"Is that really what you want?"

"Kids, you mean?" She looked up sharply. "With my job and so many lives on the line, why would you ask me that now?"

Shaking his head, he poured the ready-to-feed formula into a bottle liner. "Being a special agent, I mean. Is that really what you want?"

"It's all I've *ever* wanted," she said defensively before turning away from him to nuzzle the fuzzy softness of the baby's head.

"You sure you weren't just raised to want it? Following somebody else's—"

She spun around, eyes narrowed. "Do people ever ask *you* that? Imply that being a Ranger is some sort of crime against your masculine nature?"

"Being a Ranger *is* my nature."

"And being a special agent's mine. It's in the blood. It comes first. Always has and always will."

He shook his head. "I'm sorry. I didn't mean to—"

A knock at the door saved him from making an even bigger fool of himself. Flipping back into Ranger mode, he went to check the peephole, his weapon instantly in hand.

Shannon's thoughts flashed back to the motel, to the men who'd tried to shoot their way in. With no weapon at her disposal, though, she instead saw to the infant's safety, taking him into the bedroom.

"It's Doc—my medic friend," Rafe called as he unlocked the dead bolt a moment later. "You can bring the kiddo back out."

Shannon emerged, and Rafe introduced her to a man in his early thirties, with a runner's build, sandy, short hair and what appeared to be burn scars covering his left jaw and chin. The arm on the same side was mostly covered by a compression sleeve.

"Before you start up," the newcomer told her, "yeah, it hurt a lot, but I don't want your pity or to hear you say you're sorry. Not unless you had something to do with the IED that did it."

Taken aback by his bluntness, she said, "I was about to say thanks for taking care of me yesterday."

"Did it for the captain," he said dismissively, his deep brown eyes giving her a look of cold appraisal.

The baby squirmed and fussed—no doubt chilled by Doc's personality. If one could call it that.

"Bottle should be warm enough," Rafe told her. "You want me to take him?"

"I've got this." Shannon stepped around the counter and into the kitchen. Balancing the baby in one arm, she pulled the bottle from the pan of hot water where it had been warming and tested the milk's temperature. Judging it acceptable, she said, "Here you go, big boy."

The baby latched on with a will, his cries giving

way to enthusiastic suckling as Shannon listened to the men's conversation.

"Came to tell you, Captain," Doc said, "me and Deuce got a lead on the kid's identity. Last name's Michaels, we think."

"How'd you come up with that?" Rafe asked.

"Well, he's still got his umbilical stump, but it's about ready to come off. That puts him at about ten to fourteen days old. Deuce did a search, looking for news items on murders matching your sister's M.O.—got a hit in next to no time, killing just outside Jacksonville." Raising the laptop bag he had carried in, Doc asked Rafe, "Want to see a picture of the mother? I swear, the kid looks like her."

Rafe shook his head, teeth gritted, before spitting out, "That's another woman dead, another woman murdered after Lissa. I should have moved faster. Should have stopped Powers before he destroyed another family."

"Yeah, and we should've nailed bin Laden years ago," Doc said. "But you didn't, and we haven't. So shut up about it and let's do something about it…sir."

"And here I thought you only hated women," Shannon murmured.

Doc's attempt at a grin made a ghoulish mask of his scar tissue. "Oh, hell no. I pretty much hate everybody these days." With a glance at Rafe, he added, "But I pay back those I owe."

"You don't owe me anything. I was just doing my job."

"The hell you were." Doc looked at Shannon while hooking his thumb in Rafe's direction. "This idiot *officer* took two bullets dragging my ass out of hell. It's not something I forget, even if I do want to shove those medals of his down his throat for the *favor* most days."

"Like you could, without a whole platoon to help you," Rafe said offhandedly. "So what about this family? Did the father survive? Or did they kill him, too, to get to her?"

"Nope," Doc answered. "The dad wasn't home when it happened, and they left the three-year-old alive in the room where she was napping."

Rafe blew out a breath. "Thank God for that, at least."

"You hear that?" Shannon told the baby, whose eyes were growing dreamy, his suckling less intense. "You have a big sister to help watch out for you."

Just as her brother Steve had watched over her, even if he was annoying about it at times. And how had she repaid him? By vanishing, scaring him out of his wits, and then sleeping with the enemy—even if they hadn't managed to consummate the act.

She looked away, face burning, and told herself it didn't matter. Even if she couldn't stop remembering how gently and how selflessly Rafe had given her a gift of pleasure.

"So how are we going to get him home?" Rafe asked.

"You leave that to me'n Deuce. We'll drop the kid somewhere safe—a fire station or a hospital—and attach a note with all the information the cops'll need to start the process."

"You can't just return him to the family directly?" Rafe asked.

Shannon stepped in and explained, "That sounds like a nice idea, but it would be too hard on everybody to let them see him until they test the DNA to be sure. The authorities will make it a priority, though. Shouldn't take more than a few days to get confirmation. And when you write that note, you be sure to mention Dominic Powers by name. That'll at least get the authorities moving in the right direction."

Rafe seemed to consider before nodding. "I agree, the time's right to tip them off."

"So is the kid done with his bottle?" Doc asked.

Shannon wanted to say no, to tell the scarred medic to take a hike. The baby had let go of the nipple and fallen asleep in her arms, nestling so close he felt like an extension of her body, and she didn't want to give him up.

"I'll get his stuff together," Rafe said, and from the stiffness of his shoulders as he turned away, Shannon guessed that he, too, felt a bit of her reluctance.

"This part's good news, right?" Doc asked. "This is what you wanted?"

"Best news I've had in a—" When Rafe glanced at the medic's scarred face, something in it stopped him. "There's more, isn't there? Something else you're keeping from me."

Shannon looked up sharply, studying the medic as his gaze slid away.

"I should've made Deuce tell you. Would've, if I hadn't had to check on *her* again." A resentful sneer on his lips, Doc jerked his head in her direction.

"Made Deuce tell me what?" Rafe's voice flattened like a piece of hammered metal. "Don't jerk me around. Just tell me straight out, soldier, and look me in the eyes."

At the unmistakable order, the medic's gaze snapped up to meet his. "Your brother-in-law's dead. Flatlined earlier this morning in the trauma center."

While Shannon gasped, Rafe burst out, *"What?"*

"I'm sorry to report, sir," Doc said, his gaze still glued on Rafe's, "Garrett Smith died from multiple gunshot wounds he received yesterday after three men kicked down the door of your hotel room and made off with whatever they could carry."

"That's impossible," Rafe said, glancing at the newscast, which had moved on to an entertainment update on the latest misbehavior of some spoiled starlet. "It would have been all over the news."

"Looks like the feds were sitting on the info, but you can't keep something like that quiet for long," Doc claimed just before, as if on cue, a large red "Breaking News" banner flashed across the screen, followed by an exterior shot of the economy hotel where they'd been staying.

Rafe cursed, turning his back to them. Heart aching, Shannon carried the baby closer to the TV and turned up the volume. The voiceover reported that three unidentified men had somehow slipped past the distracted clerk before entering the elevator. Minutes later a male guest, as yet unidentified, had been attacked inside his third-floor room. Taken to a local trauma center with multiple gunshot wounds, he had died earlier today.

By the time the story ended, Shannon felt an icy numbness radiating from her core. Rafe sank into one of the chairs with his elbows on his spread knees, his head in his hands, and his jaw and eyes clenched tightly. Shannon wanted to go to him, to say something, do something, to ease his misery, but instinct warned her not to touch him or to try to speak to him, not now.

Instead, she turned to ask Doc, "What else can you tell us?"

"A local cop my buddy Deuce knows told him there's

security footage from the lobby and the hallways. Three white guys, on the young side, with automatic weapons and camo hoods. Not sure how they managed it, but they slipped inside when the lobby was empty and the clerk had stepped away from the desk."

"Camo hoods?" asked Shannon, convinced Rafe had been right to guess at the hackers' involvement. "They're *playing*. Playing 'Battle Bloodcraft.'"

"They're what? You mean like— Yeah, you're right. The warrior tribes wear hoods."

"You've played it?"

Doc gave her a dark look. "I've had a lot of time on my hands this past year."

Tired of his attitude, she snapped, "Maybe you should use some of it to work on finding Rafe's niece."

"For what?" Rafe ground out, his voice shaking with emotion. "To take her to her parents' gravesides? Or to Garrett's mother, who beat him so badly, he could barely bring himself to send her a card at Christmas? Or maybe her foster parents can bring her to visit me in Leavenworth? For all I know, she's better off where she is, with two loving parents who have no idea what Powers did to get her."

Taking over for him, Shannon told Doc, "Just help us find the baby. We'll worry later about what's best for her."

"Don't know if there's anything we *can* do," the medic said, his brown eyes intense, "but you have my word—there's absolutely nothing I won't do to help Captain Lyons find his niece."

CONSUELO'S DARK EYES WELLED as she rocked and sang to *la bebé*. In her home country of Nicaragua, such a beautiful child would be extravagantly loved and cared for, passed from one eager set of arms to the next as everyone, from grandparents to aunts and uncles, older siblings, cousins and godparents, clamored to christen the newest family member with welcoming hugs and kisses.

Unlike in this *casa de locos*—this madhouse—where the young *señora* loved nothing but the memory of a white rat of *un perro* and *el señor* thought of little but convincing the public he was younger than his years. Had someone told him a young starlet of a wife and a new baby would erase some of his creases—the damage of five decades filled with sun and sin and cigarettes? *Diós* knew, the man had no real thoughts of his own, only those that he was given by those paid to stroke his ego.

I will protect you, precious baby. I will rock and kiss and hold you. But since her diagnosis, Consuelo couldn't say for how much longer.

She hadn't said a word to her employer, hadn't said a word to anyone about her cancer. Because she had no insurance to pay for the treatment, and she knew the Worths would dismiss her the moment they found out, would have her quietly deported if she made a peep of protest.

Besides, she missed the loved ones she had left behind so many years before in her native country, so many loved ones who had passed on long ago. She would just as soon be finished working for these most pampered and foolish of *Americanos* and return to her *familia* in the only way she could.

But for the sake of this poor child, Consuelo prayed the end might come a little later than she'd once hoped.

For without her in attendance, this tiny innocent would be left without a single champion in a household incapable of love.

Chapter Seventeen

On some level, it all registered. Doc's and Shannon's quiet conversation, the reluctance in her eyes as she lowered the sleeping baby—most likely the Michaels child—into the carrier.

On another, it was only white noise, a background murmur that failed to penetrate the roaring in Rafe's ears. The unvoiced howl of rage, of grief, of pure frustration, tearing through him. Of an anguish so raw he had no idea what to do with it.

Without a word to either Doc or Shannon, Rafe went to the master bedroom and closed the door behind him, unwilling to face the others as he fought to wrap his head around this latest loss.

He never should have taken Garrett with him. Should have relied instead on phone or internet connections to communicate whatever information he needed. Instead, Rafe had given in to Garrett's pleas, then refused to listen to him after the first raid, when he had warned Rafe that he wasn't up for this, that he needed to go home where he belonged.

Why the hell didn't you let him? Figure out some way to get along without his help? Cursing himself, Rafe paced the room's cramped confines, his skin feeling tight to the point of bursting with the remorse simmering inside him.

He might have saved Shannon from an uncertain fate on the street, but there was nothing, absolutely nothing, he could do to fix Garrett or the mess that he himself had made of this mission.

He whirled around, glaring as Shannon knocked, then opened the door.

"Sorry to disturb you," she said, "but I thought you should know, Doc's just left with the baby. Or did you want to say goodbye? I could probably still catch him."

"Garrett was right," Rafe murmured. "Bringing you into this has caused nothing but more problems."

Standing in the doorway, she studied him with the intensity of a woman sizing up a swarming wasps' nest, deciding the best way to neutralize the threat without getting stung.

"From the very first," he accused, "you started sowing seeds of distrust, implying Garrett was somehow wrapped up in Lissa's murder. If it weren't for you, I might have listened after he was hurt—might've trusted him enough to send him home before he got killed."

"I know you're angry. Upset. Looking for someone else to blame. But it won't help—"

"What *will* help, now that they're both dead?" he asked, his voice more sad than angry. "What's going to make the slightest difference now that both Lissa and Garrett—now that I've screwed things up so badly that—"

"Beating yourself up won't help, either. Garrett wanted to be part of this. Except when he was in so much pain that he could scarcely think, he insisted on it." She took a step toward him, compassion filling her eyes. "And he had every right, Rafe. Amber *is* his daughter."

"A daughter who needed him alive to raise her."

"What would you say to one of your men," she asked, taking first one step and then another, until only inches lay between them, "if he wasted time laying blaming after a setback instead of refocusing on his mission? What would the Lion, the decorated war hero, have to say about a man like—"

"Do you think I've forgotten? Forgotten for a single second that my niece is out there somewhere?"

"You *are* forgetting, Rafe. Forgetting the men risking everything to help you."

"I don't want them helping." His gaze found the bruise half-hidden by her silky brown bangs, then touched on the others marking her arms, all evidence of how close he'd come to losing her, too. "I won't have anyone else hurt. Especially not you."

"I told you before, you're stuck with me until this is over. Until we've succeeded."

"I'll handle the operation myself from now on, the way I should have from the start."

"Listen, Rafe, I know you're upset. I don't blame you. But you need a partner in this. A partner you can count on."

"And you need to take a hike—now. There's a restaurant a block from here. Go there and ask them to let you make a phone call. Can you handle that? The walk, I mean. Can you make it?"

She crossed her arms and glared at him. "When I leave, I leave with you in custody. It's the only way I can go back."

"You'll leave now. Empty-handed."

"So that's it?" Her brows shot higher, her face

incredulous. "After everything we've gone through, everything we've— I'm just supposed to walk away now, no hard feelings?"

"You're entitled to hard feelings. I abducted you off the street, then beat you black and blue."

"You never—"

Slowly and deliberately, he nodded toward her bruises. "I did that, Shannon. To force your cooperation."

She shook her head. "No way am I doing that. Blaming you to save my career—if that's even possible at this point."

"Suit yourself," he told her. "But the offer stands, in case you change your mind." *And if I survive this, I* will *find you. I'll surrender to you and you alone.*

"Rafe…" Her voice straining, she reached to touch his hand. "If I leave now I—"

"You reminded me of my duty. I'm reminding you of yours. Take a walk. Clear your head, Special Agent. Remember your priorities, that badge that means so much, your brother."

"Rafe," she pleaded. "I want to help you do this."

"My life, your life—the life of anyone who's worth a damn—isn't about what we want. It's about honor and integrity, about keeping vows and honoring our family. I would never…would never have let myself come to… to respect you if I didn't believe you feel the same way." He touched her then, laying a finger on her breast above her pounding heart.

As he did, a single tear trembled on her lower lashes. A tear that told him she was every bit the woman he had judged her to be.

A woman he had no choice except to turn away.

"All right," Shannon swallowed past a lump to tell him. "If that's the way you want it, I'm g-going for that walk now." She had other responsibilities beyond Rafe Lyons. Responsibilities she had neglected far too long. To her brother, to her duty, to the badge she had been so proud to carry during her brief tenure with the bureau.

Turning from him, she walked toward the front door. Toward safety, freedom and every possibility that life without the Ranger offered.

She heard him behind her, in the soft padding of his footsteps, the hard breathing that spelled out some inner struggle. Though he remained steadfastly silent, she felt the weight of his expectation, a weight so solid and so heavy, it crushed the air from her lungs.

At the door, she hesitated, her fingers wrapping around the cool knob, her heart pounding in her chest. And in that instant she wanted more than anything to turn around, to lose herself—lose both of them—in kisses that could only culminate in the consummation her body ached for.

Instead she did as he had asked, walking out to find the restaurant he'd described, to find a way to make the call duty demanded before her will to leave him crumbled.

FREED OF ALL ENCUMBRANCES—that was how Rafe knew he should feel. With no tiny infant slowing him, no injured woman to consider—not even the burden of his grieving brother-in-law—he packed his few remaining belongings quickly before making his way down the metal staircase and out to yet another replacement vehicle, which Doc had brought him last night, an older Taurus the same dark gray as the gathering storm clouds and his own thunderous mood.

You're a Ranger, born to lead the way. So think like

one. Forget them—all of them. And most of all, forget going after her.

Because as much—and as willingly—as Shannon had chosen to help him up to this point, he couldn't let her make the sacrifice that he had for his sister's baby. And most of all, he couldn't risk sacrificing *her.*

It was time to move out now, without looking behind him. To do whatever he must to find out where and whether Dominic Powers had moved his operation.

A restless wind came off the nearby water, whistling through the palm fronds, and ruffling the leaves and peeling red bark of the gumbo limbo trees nearby. Oppressively humid, the warm air seemed primed for an explosion, hungry for the spark that would ignite a summer storm.

Feeling just as combustible, Rafe revved the car's engine and threw it into gear. Though he didn't regret a moment he'd spent tending the Michaels baby and watching over Shannon, he knew he'd already lost his best chance to trace Powers. By this time, there would be little left to do except track down any loose-lipped packers, shippers or rental agents he could find, relying on persuasion, deception and what was left of the two grand he'd had on him yesterday after leaving the rest of their cash with Garrett at the hotel.

Garrett... Regret shafted across Rafe's consciousness like lightning, and he struggled to shake off his losses, to put them out of his mind. To focus on what he still had: the wits and skills and contacts he had developed throughout his years as a Ranger.

With one last look around the two-story condo unit's palm-lined lot, he backed out of his parking space and headed out of town in the direction of the Palm Beach villa he was nearly certain Powers had abandoned.

Toward it and away from his last point of contact with a woman he already missed—a woman he feared he would ache for as long as he drew breath.

SHANNON BARELY MANAGED to say hello when her brother interrupted.

"Shannon! Where are you? I've been going crazy—all of us have. Working day and night tracking sightings up and down the Florida coast."

"It's so good to hear your voice, Steve. I'm sorry—really sorry you've been worried." Cupping her hand over the receiver, she glanced at the Seafood Shack's sole waitress, a wide-hipped black woman who was half-heartedly wiping down tables during the midafternoon lull. Eavesdropping, Shannon suspected—concerned or simply curious about the younger woman who had limped in and begged to use the phone.

"Has he hurt you?" There was no mistaking the distress in Steve's question, the toll his inability to protect his only sibling had taken on him in the days since her abduction. "You sound... Your voice sounds strained."

"I'll be fine," Shannon said, struggling to remain calm. "But there's something I have to—"

"Where are you?" he asked again. "The caller ID's coming up as 'private number.'"

That's because I blocked it before calling, to slow you down long enough so I can get away. "I can't tell you that, Steve." She wasn't even sure where Rafe had taken her. Judging from the rows of modest-looking condos along a waterfront still dotted with the kind of Old Florida "beach shacks" passed down through gen-erations, they were some distance from Palm Beach, but she'd hadn't yet made an effort to pinpoint her location. "Right now, though, I need you to listen to—"

"It's Lyons, isn't it? The Ranger's the one who took you. He's forcing you to call. Let me talk to him. Right now."

"Please, I'm asking for your help, if you'll quit interrupting."

"What help, Shannon? Because other than getting you somewhere safe for debriefing—"

"Quiet," she snapped, refusing to allow him to play the all-knowing big brother. The "real" agent in the family, as opposed to the tagalong little sister trailing in his wake. Cutting another look toward the waitress, she whispered, "There's not much time if you want a piece of the monster behind the Madonna Murders."

"You have a suspect? Or does Lyons think he has one?"

"He does, and I believe him. I've seen the evidence firsthand. It's an attorney out of Houston, a man trafficking in stolen infants. Already we've recovered one—"

"Don't tell me you've let Lyons con you into helping him. He's a felon, Shannon. Your kidnapping alone is enough to send him to Leavenworth for life. And if you're involving yourself unofficially, snatching infants—"

"I went with Rafe willingly," she blurted, without quite understanding why. Could her lie be enough to save him—to keep a man willing to sacrifice his freedom to return lost babies to their rightful families from facing prison?

"Yeah, right. We have witnesses, Shannon. People saw you tased and thrown into a waiting vehicle."

"Listen, Steve," she told him, tears burning in her

eyes. "Returning infants to their rightful families is a duty, not a crime."

"You may be right about that last part, but only *if* it's done through legal channels."

"Oh, sure. Spend days or weeks fighting through the paperwork while the kidnapper auctions those babies off to heaven knows where—someplace out of the country, for all we know." Shannon realized she was sounding more like Rafe than the responsible team player she had always been, but these were special circumstances, not a time to trot out rules. "This could be a huge break. Now are you going to help me, or are you going to sit and lecture?"

"Have you lost your mind? Is Lyons holding you at gunpoint? Or has he used other means of coercion?"

"He hasn't hurt me," she insisted, anger turning up the heat in her voice and drawing a concerned look from the waitress.

"Listen, Shannon. You may not be aware of this, but Special Forces soldiers are trained to exploit whatever resources they find in their environment," he warned, as if she'd hadn't been the one to fill in her own team on this bit of background research. "The only thing that matters to a Ranger on a mission is accomplishing his objective. Whether he's hurt you, conned you or had the balls to try seducing a special agent, you need to get it through your head you're nothing to him. Nothing but a means to whatever end he's got in mind."

"He's not angling for anything for himself. He's a good man, an honorable man who only wants to bring his niece home. Wants to get all the babies to their families. Once that's finished, I'll talk him into turning himself in."

She still believed she could return to help him and

eventually get him safely into custody, no matter what he'd said in his grief-fueled attempts to push her away.

"I can't believe this. I can hear it in your voice. You really think you're in love with him, don't you?" Disgust resonated in Steve's deep voice.

"Who said anything about love?" she fired back, as Rafe's face flashed through her mind.

"I thought you were smarter than this, better than this—and way more committed to your career."

"Isn't doing the right thing for those families more important than any job?"

"I can't even imagine what Uncle Lloyd or Dad would have to say about the way you're twisting—"

She slammed the phone down out of sheer frustration, convinced she would never get Steve's help in tracking down Powers. And stung by the suspicion that he could be right—that she had fallen for a man so skillful that even his seemingly selfless request for her to leave had been carefully scripted to deceive her.

Ridiculous. She knew that, would bet her life that the Rafe she'd seen reacting to Garrett's murder and her beating had been the genuine article. So how was it that Steve could so quickly twist things around to make her feel so inadequate, so incompetent—so *judged* and found wanting, the way she'd always felt with Uncle Lloyd?

"You all right, honey?" The waitress drew near enough that Shannon could read the crab-shaped tag pinned to her ample bosom identifying her as *CeeCee.* "If you need help, I got a card behind the counter from some nice ladies, run the local shelter. For women with man troubles."

Shaking her head, Shannon thanked her for the phone's use before hurrying back outside, where a lion's growl of thunder echoed against the threatening sky. Hoping to beat the rain, she started walking, retracing her path back toward the condo. Back toward the most dangerous "man trouble" of her life.

Occasional gaps between the condo buildings offered glimpses of the roiling, white-capped water, a sea gone as ominous as her mood. Hurrying her pace, she made it to the Gulf Stream Vacation Condos and hauled her tired, aching body up to the unit marked 4B.

A unit where, as she had both feared and half expected, no one answered her increasingly loud knocks. Because Rafe had wasted no time putting distance between the two of them.

A distance she was powerless to close.

Chapter Eighteen

The rain came and went throughout the afternoon, at times a gentle patter on Rafe's windshield and at others an angry hiss against the old Taurus's metal body. Before he made Palm Beach, he drove through several storm bands and discovered, thanks to the static-plagued radio, that he'd somehow missed the news of a tropical depression developing off the coast, where it was quickly building into what would soon be a named storm.

Because of the noise, he nearly missed the sound of his ringing cell phone—a sound that startled him, since only Garrett had this number. Quickly he pulled over, the old Ford splashing its way between a Ferrari and a Porsche in front of a Worth Avenue jewelry store with a huge Rolex logo in the window.

The caller ID offered him no clue, so he answered, his heartbeat drumming, "Who is this?"

No one spoke, and Rafe reminded himself that Garrett was dead, that the only people who might have recovered his phone or somehow come up with this number were either his killers or the authorities, trying to track down next of kin. Or trying to find Rafe, if they had already identified the dead man.

"You call me for a reason?" he asked. "Because otherwise you're wasting my time *and* yours."

Someone began speaking. A man's voice, but so soft Rafe couldn't make out the words.

"Could you repeat that and speak up?" Rafe raised his own voice. "Can't hear you with this rain."

"You should *thank* the rain, dude," the caller told him, his words louder, clearer, and the voice young. "This storm parked off the coast has been keeping a certain douchebag of our mutual acquaintance from sailing out of Palm Beach."

"From where?"

When the caller named the marina and slip number, Rafe committed them to memory, then followed up with, "Who *is* this?"

"A friend… An old friend of your brother-in-law's. You can call me Zero, if that suits you."

"A friend who turned on him and killed him? That the kind of friend you are, Zero?"

"*I* didn't kill him." Resentment crept into the caller's tone, as if he were offended by the accusation.

"But you know who did, don't you?" Rafe asked, now certain he was dealing with one of Garrett's hacker buddies.

As he might have expected, Zero changed the subject, saying, "You'll need to stop Powers pretty fast. He's used the yacht's onboard computer to chart a course to the Cayman Islands, where we figure he's got most of his money stashed."

"And where extraditing him back to the U.S. for a death-penalty crime would be a nightmare," Rafe murmured, though he wasn't about to let any nation's laws stand between him and the justice both Powers and the stolen babies' families had coming. "So what else can you give me? Any intel on personnel aboard? Electronic security? Anything that might prove helpful?"

"He's got a system called Cyber-Yacht. Electrified perimeter, cameras out the wazoo, GPS, intruder alarms and remote internet access."

Rafe felt a smile pulling at the corners of his mouth. "Which I assume isn't as secure from guys like you as advertised."

"Darn the luck," said the hacker with a laugh.

Rafe smiled but didn't allow this moment of camaraderie to blind him to the dangers. "So how do I know we're on the same side, Zero?"

"'Cause I got a sister, too, dude. My sister—she took care of me. Got me through the gauntlet of our mom's crazy boyfriends in one piece. If anybody ever hurt her…"

"Touching story," Rafe said, feeling more than skeptical about this call, this source, and the convenient legend of the sister-loving hacker. "Let me know when you sell it to the Hallmark Channel."

"Believe me or eff off, man. Whatever. If you hang up now, sooner or later—maybe years from now—me and my associates will find some way to stick it to that douchebag. But tell me, how many other pregnant ladies is he gonna carve up before we get to him?"

Zero had a valid point, but how could Rafe trust him? Maybe Powers himself had employed the caller? Or maybe, despite his denials, Zero was in league with those who had taken their online commando role-playing far too seriously.

But the more important question was what other options did Rafe have left? With his resources depleted and his decision to send Shannon out of harm's way, what else could he do but stake his success—his very survival—upon this slender thread?

"ARE YOU SURE YOU DON'T MIND?" Shannon asked
the driver, a balding man with creased brown skin and
a belly that pressed against the steering wheel.

"No, miss, I surely don't." As his pickup's wipers
slapped away the rain, the man who'd introduced himself as Harold smiled at her, revealing a gap between
his front teeth and dark eyes steeped in kindness. "And
even if I did, don't do a man a lick of good to come up
against my CeeCee when she call and say she got the
Lord's work that needs doin'. Leastwise, not if that man
want that good leftover pie to keep on slidin' his way."

Though Shannon was still damp from her walk
back to the Seafood Shack, his rich laughter warmed
her as much as his wife's insistence that her husband
would take her "wherever you need to get yourself safe,
honey."

"Thank you so much," she said. "Especially considering this weather."

"This little blow ain't nothing," Harold assured her.
"Don't you think another thing about it."

Shannon still wasn't certain she'd been right to insist
on returning to Palm Beach, which had turned out to be
an hour and a half's drive from their location. Even if
Rafe had driven there to look for any trace of Powers,
finding the Ranger would still be a long shot.

But she couldn't come up with a better place to look
for Rafe any more than she could imagine leaving him
to face Powers and Red Beard and heaven only knew
how many others on his own.

After a drive that seemed to last forever, Harold
turned onto Worth Avenue, South Florida's answer to
Rodeo Drive.

"Will you look at this, miss. Lord have mercy," he

said, his gaze swinging from one side to the other, his eyes wide as he took in the sights.

Shannon pretended interest, gawking like a tourist at the Italian architecture and the neat rows of carefully tended palm trees. Everywhere she looked, signs caught her attention: Gucci, Saks and Chanel, Hermes, Tiffany & Co. and Rolex, along with names she didn't recognize. She would have traded the contents of every overpriced store for a single glimpse of Rafe.

Barely noticing the dark sedan with the tinted windows that had pulled in behind them, she said, "Remember, I told you my friend lives a few more blocks off the beach."

Slightly shamefaced, Harold admitted, "That's right. It's the devil lurin' me to look at what I can't afford and don't need—say, is that big white car a *Rolls Royce?*"

"Sure looks like it," she said, grinning at the wonder in his voice. "But I'd probably better get to my friend's place and let you get home to your pie."

Shannon directed him to turn, then kept her eyes peeled for someplace she could ask to be dropped. Focused as she was, she never noticed that the dark sedan had taken the same left, following them at a distance.

"You need to call first?"

"It'll be fine. Um—I think it's down this street," she told him, wanting to get out before she had to tell this nice man any more lies. "Yes, that's it—on the right."

Following her directions, Harold pulled to a stop in front of an attractive yellow town house trimmed in white. "You sure your friend's gonna welcome you?"

Shannon nodded. "Probably after another lecture about ignoring her advice and picking the wrong man, as usual. But she's my best friend. She'll help me. And then I'll send you money for your gas."

"Forget about that," he said thoughtfully. "Just do me one favor. Listen to your friend and stay away from bad men. Otherwise, one of 'em's likely to beat you all the way dead next time, instead of only half."

Don't I know it. After thanking him profusely, Shannon climbed out of the truck and waved goodbye. Unfortunately, Harold didn't leave right away but watched her until she had hurried through the gate and stepped onto the front porch.

When she pretended to ring the bell, he drove away at last.

Inside the town house, what sounded like a pack of rabid lapdogs yapped furiously, having detected her intrusion. Leaving the porch before anyone human responded, she started down the sidewalk, her mind sifting through ideas of how to connect with a Ranger who did not want to be found.

That was when she finally noticed the Jaguar parked along the curb a few doors ahead. With all its windows, even the front, darkly tinted, she couldn't see a driver, but the refined purr of the big engine convinced her someone must be inside.

Belatedly remembering that she had seen the car behind them earlier, Shannon realized the driver must be watching her and waiting for her to come toward him. She quickly spun on her heel, her mouth drying and her heartbeat racing, as she hurried toward an alley that cut between town houses.

Just as she reached it, Red Beard burst out at her, murder in his eyes.

Screaming, Shannon turned and ran. Fighting through the pain of her injuries, she avoided both Red Beard and the sedan she'd suspected he'd come out of, where she feared an accomplice might be waiting. From the yellow town house, she heard the lapdogs' frenzy, but no one came to help her or stuck a head outdoors to shout—not even when she heard two cracks behind her. Gunfire.

"Hold it!" Red Beard shouted, huffing hard on her heels, closing in on her with incredible speed considering his bulk. "Stop right there, bitch, or the next one's right through your heart."

Reminding herself how hard it was to hit a moving target and how little mercy she could expect from her pursuer, Shannon cut hard to her left, praying her luck would hold as she darted between parked cars and dashed into the street.

Tires squealed, brakes screeched and a horn blared as an SUV nearly struck her. Shannon stopped short just in time, her legs so weak, she nearly tumbled to the pavement. But gasping for breath and hampered by her prior injuries, she was too slow to recover and start running again.

As the driver honked one last time and roared off, a hand clamped down on Shannon's shoulder. She struggled to jab with her elbow and kick backward, but this time her trembling legs did collapse beneath her, and there was nothing—nothing in the world—she could do to stop the man she knew meant to kill her from forcing her inside the Jaguar that glided to a stop beside them.

I'm sorry, Rafe. So sorry. I should never have left you in the first place.

Chapter Nineteen

With the wind whipping and the thick clouds covering the moon, the night was as black as the hard pit Dominic Powers called a heart.

Before this night is over, I'll carve it out and feed it to you, if that's what it takes to find those babies.

Rafe sat beneath a burned-out security light several docks distant from the one where Powers's luxury yacht was berthed. Churning wavelets slapped at his dangling legs, and thunder growled as rain hissed off every surface, from wood to fiberglass to the roiling water.

It was an ugly night for diving, an even uglier night to attempt it without a partner to back him up. As lightning strobed above, a memory of Shannon flashed through his mind, followed by a crushing sense of loss.

"Hell, Rafe, pull yourself together," he murmured, wrenching her from his thoughts to focus on the mission. A mission he swore he would return from to assure his niece's future.

Though walking aboard the one-hundred-twelve-foot, six-million-dollar *Cut Above* would have been the more convenient option, Rafe suspected that Powers, in his eagerness to leave town, had his crew and what remained of his security team onboard. And even after the hacker calling himself Zero knocked out the security cameras,

Powers would still surely have at least one man, maybe two, watching the dock in case anyone approached.

Though it was possible other eyes might be monitoring the swim platform just below the aft deck, Rafe was betting Powers's team wouldn't be expecting a swimmer on a night so rough that the yacht was pitching wildly in its berth.

Rafe wasn't thrilled about the prospect, either, especially since he would be using only basic snorkeling equipment, rather than a tank and wetsuit. But his water training—including "drown-proofing" that had required him to bob, float and swim with both his hands and feet bound—had left him confident he could make it if he avoided getting tangled in ropes, trash or other obstacles while swimming clothed through the darkness.

He'd picked up a dive light along with a mask and fins, but turning on the underwater flashlight would put him at risk for being spotted. Resolving to use it only if absolutely necessary, he hooked it to his belt beside the sheath containing his carbon fiber knife and a pistol he had carefully wrapped in multiple layers of locking plastic storage bags.

"Here goes everything," he said, slipping off the dock and into the water, which he found pleasantly warm, despite the day's rain. Grateful not to have to add hypothermia to his list of worries, he started swimming blind, relying on his sense of direction and physical conditioning to carry him through.

Churned up by the storm, the powerful currents would have drowned a weaker swimmer. Brutally insistent, they washed him off course several times, forcing him to pop up and check his bearings. But the *Cut Above* was like a beacon, its onboard lights marking it as one of the few occupied boats in this part of the marina.

Probably most other crews and owners had chosen to avoid the jostling and stay on land this evening, but Rafe doubted any other owners were as desperate to set sail as soon as the weather cleared. Or half as nervous about the possibility that the two intruders who had driven them from the villa might gather reinforcements, then corner and attack them here.

Bet you're not expecting a force of one, by water.

Submerging to complete his journey, Rafe reached the stern swim deck without incident. After a quick scan revealed no watchers, he hesitated for a moment, treading water and praying that the anonymous hacker who had claimed to want to help him had disabled the yacht's security system as promised.

Pushing himself up onto the deck, Rafe had the knife in his teeth and the dry pistol in hand in an instant. But there was no shout of alarm, no gunfire—not a single indication his arrival had been noted.

That may have been, Rafe realized less than a minute later, because the occupants were all distracted by the pandemonium he heard erupting somewhere inside. Angry male voices preceded a heavy thump and running footsteps—but what had Rafe racing toward the chaos was the pain and terror in an unmistakably female scream.

FOR A FEW FRANTIC MOMENTS Shannon honestly thought she might make it. Twisting free of her two interrogators, she raced out of the stateroom where she'd been held, then rammed the chair leg she had broken beneath the door behind her to lock them in.

As Red Beard's first powerful kicks shook the jammed door, she turned and raced away, praying she wouldn't run into any more of Powers's men.

With no idea how far offshore they might be—Red Beard had chloroformed her in the Jaguar, and she had no idea how long she'd been out—her only thought was getting to a radio or cell phone to call for offshore helicopter backup. Stopping in the galley, she desperately pulled out drawers in search of a knife, but Powers and Red Beard burst in only steps behind her, both men pointing guns straight at her chest.

"You're only making things worse," Powers said coolly, though his reddened face and heaving chest belied his calm. "All I need is some basic information on your partner. Tell me what I want to know and you have nothing more to fear."

Because I'll be dead, Shannon understood, using the last of her strength to hurl a platter at them before Red Beard slammed her facedown over the counter, twisting her right arm behind her and deliberately pulling back her index and middle fingers.

"Teach you," he said, "to run away from me."

She screamed as bone cracked audibly, sending neon streaks across her blacked-out vision.

When she could see again, she found herself on her knees among the broken shards of the monogrammed platter. When she looked up, Powers was standing over her, his 9 mm custom pistol pointed straight between her eyes.

"I grow tired of asking," he said. "Tell me what I want to know, or my crew will be scrubbing your brains off the cabinetry."

So she was going to die. Now, with the secret of Rafe's name and his mission unspoken. With his face flashing through her mind, she wondered, was the Ranger close now, or had Powers's yacht left him far behind?

I'm so sorry, Rafe, but whenever you do get to

him, please avenge me. Avenge my death along with Lissa's....

The pounding of her heart morphed into the sound of the pounding footsteps of three men in white uniforms, who came running to investigate the noise.

"Prepare to cast off," Powers ordered, dropping the muzzle of his pistol a few inches. "We're not waiting any longer."

The news that they were still docked—far closer to help than she'd imagined—gave Shannon the courage to make one last-ditch effort. "Please—you have to stop him, or you'll be accessories to murder. I'm a federal agent. The government will hunt you down like dogs if I'm killed. They'll stop at nothing to punish anyone involved in the death of one of their own."

Ignoring her, the oldest of the three, a trim, mustachioed man whose olive skin contrasted with his crisp uniform, kept his gaze riveted to Powers's. "But, sir, this system's blown up faster than the weather service forecast. It's a tropical storm already, and they're saying it could be a full-blown hurricane by morning."

Powers scowled at him as though the conditions were his fault. "Are you telling me we can't get through it?"

"I'm telling you it'll be rough going before we clear the worst of it. As for whether or not we make it, that's in the hands of God, as always," the crewman answered, his gaze still carefully avoiding Shannon's eyes.

"How can you call on God, then let this man keep killing?" she shouted at him. At her invocation of the holy name, the three crewmen exchanged uncomfortable glances, encouraging her to press even harder. "They've killed pregnant women for their babies. Wives, daughters, sisters, with families who loved them. Did you know that? They plunged their knives into their abdomens and sliced them open like animals so—"

Red Beard backhanded her so quickly that she was flat on the deck before she knew what happened, her cheekbone throbbing.

"We've all heard enough of your lies," he said.

"How do you sleep nights, you psycho?" she hissed, but she couldn't be sure if he heard, for he'd left her too weak and dizzy to lift her head.

Powers told his crewmen, "We're leaving right away. Now go see to your duties if you want to keep your jobs."

The uniformed men filed out, leaving her with Red Beard and Powers. With her vision swimming, she could barely see them glaring down at her.

"I might have my share of regrets," Powers told her, "but seeing the last of you won't be among them. Whoever you really are, you've caused me a great deal of trouble. Forced me to uproot myself from a comfortable existence, to abandon several very lucrative business arrangements already in progress…"

Summoning the last of her strength, Shannon glared into those soulless blue eyes and delivered what she fully believed might be her final words. *"Business arrangements? Is that how you like to think of them? Do you really believe that paying others to bloody their hands on your account washes your soul clean?"*

"What? For the last time, who are you? And wherever did you hear such filthy lies?"

"Oh, it's *all* over the internet. I saw somebody tweeting about it just this morning," she managed to say, hoping to provoke them into delivering a quick death. "Oh, wait, that was *me.* Sending out emails with my evidence to every news outlet and law enforcement agency I could find a link for."

"Enough!" shouted Powers, the pistol shaking in his hand. Apparently unwilling to personally pull the trigger, he turned his empty eyes toward Red Beard's. "Just get her out of my sight. Do whatever you want with her. And when you're finished, be sure to leave her body with the others for our burial at sea."

Red Beard's smile froze her to the marrow. "You're assuming, boss, that I plan to leave enough of her to bury."

Chapter Twenty

Following the sound of the feminine scream he had heard, Rafe burst into the galley, where a man matching Paloma's description of Dominic Powers was pouring himself a glass of Chablis.

Gaping at the sight of the armed man charging toward him, Powers dropped both glass and bottle to reach for something in his waistband. Before he could get to it, Rafe struck him like a guided missile, plowing into Powers as the other man screamed, "Security!"

They hit the deck, Rafe landing on top of Powers, whose breath whooshed from his lungs in a pained explosion. Struggling to recover, he stood no chance of getting the drop on the Ranger, who frisked and disarmed him with brisk efficiency before tucking Powers's pistol into his own waistband. By the time Powers noisily sucked in another lungful, Rafe produced a zip tie, rolled the murderous attorney onto his belly and bound his wrists behind him.

With that threat neutralized, he listened, trying to gauge whether Powers's outcry had set his men into motion. Hearing nothing—at least not yet—Rafe rolled the smaller man back over and pointed his knife into the ashen face.

Rafe could scarcely believe this frightened man, with

his bulging eyes and gaping fish mouth, was the same animal who had beaten Shannon so savagely—or commanded her abuse—the same beast who had ordered Lissa's execution as if he were ordering a product from a catalog. Who might even now have another woman here for the same purpose.

"Where is she?" Rafe demanded. "Where's the woman I heard screaming? Tell me now or I swear, you're about to lose an eye. Let's make it *this one*."

He used the knife's tip to prick the skin below Powers's left eye, though the man had reflexively squeezed both shut and squealed, "No! You can't. Don't cut me!"

Rafe noted with satisfaction the damp patch spreading over the man's crotch. Good. Let him know how it felt to be terrified, defenseless. Let the bastard feel some measure of his victims' desperation.

"Double or nothing," Rafe told him. "Tell me where the woman is—or I'm carving out both eyes now."

"He took her to the starboard stateroom to finish her!" Powers bleated. "That bitch is your partner, isn't she?"

"My *partner?*" Rafe echoed, wondering if the man could actually mean Shannon. But even if she hadn't called the bureau or her brother to report in, how could that be possible? With neither money nor any form of transportation, there was no way Shannon could have beaten him here.

Horror struck him like a gut punch as he realized that despite her injuries, Shannon was clever and resourceful enough to have found her way to the yacht somehow. Instinct warned him that she must have done just that—that the screams he'd heard had been hers.

"Which way?" Rafe demanded.

Before Powers could answer, there was a clamor from

below, men shouting and scrambling just ahead of a short burst of machine-gun fire. But who was shooting? And why? Was Shannon attempting an escape?

"Please!" Powers blubbered. "Please don't cut me."

A snarl curled Rafe's lip. "Shut up and tell me which way." *And pray that Shannon's still alive for me to save.*

"It's that way." Powers jerked his head to indicate a point forward and to the right, or starboard, side. "I'll give you anything you want—I have money. Please. I'm begging you."

"I wonder if my sister begged before those bastards you sent cut her baby from her belly."

"I— It's all a mistake! I had no idea my associates were hurting anybody!"

Incensed by the obvious lie, Rafe punched the man, his fist smashing into Powers's cheekbone so hard that the back of the man's head banged against the floor. But Rafe's loss of control came at a steep price, because Powers was knocked unconscious.

Leaving him for now, Rafe rushed in the direction Powers had indicated—and prayed that the gunfire he'd heard hadn't ended Shannon's life already, that he would have a chance to tell her what was only now hitting him with the brute force of a sledgehammer. That he needed her, wanted her, even *loved* her, no matter how impossibly the odds were stacked against them.

WITH EVERY MOVE Shannon's pain grew more insistent. But this time she wouldn't blow it—she would use this opportunity to escape.

To take a chance on finding Rafe.

Red Beard had slapped a pair of cuffs on her wrists and left to check out the gunfire they'd heard from the deck below. "Don't start without me, baby. We'll get our little party going as soon as I come back," he'd promised, before rushing out and locking the stateroom behind him.

Grateful he hadn't taken time to knock her out or bind her legs, Shannon searched the room, hoping to find a bit of wire—anything she might use to pick the lock of her cuffs. For several minutes she searched high and low, pulling out drawers with her bound hands and nearly shrieking with pain when she accidentally stubbed her broken fingers. Finally she pulled a clip off a stack of papers and worked feverishly to straighten it as best she could.

Cursing her clumsiness, she dropped the paper clip several times and wondered if there was any way she would ever succeed before he came back, much less find some way out of the small, windowless stateroom. Tears of pain and frustration stood in her eyes by the time the first cuff finally popped open. But before she could cross the room, she heard someone rattling the knob.

A moment later there was a sharp crack as the door burst inward, striking the wall behind it with a bang as loud as a shot.

"Shannon!" Rafe's broad shoulders nearly filled the door frame as he rushed forward to embrace her tightly.

"Oh, Rafe." She gasped, joy and relief cut short by a jolt of pain. "Careful of my hands. I've got a couple of broken fingers. And anyway, he's coming right back."

"Who is?" Rafe pulled away to study her face, anger hardening his expression as he touched her swollen cheekbone. "Who did this? Who hurt you, Shannon?"

"It's the thug with the red beard, one of the men I

think killed your sister. He just went to check out the shooting we heard. Was that you coming aboard?"

Rafe shook his head. "Not me, but I did get to Powers. I left him out cold in the galley. But I have no idea who else is onboard who might have fired those shots, or why."

As if on cue, they heard a second round of gunfire.

"Can you walk?" Rafe asked.

Weak as she was, she nodded, her will resurrected by the sight of a face she had been certain she would never see again.

"Then let's go. Hurry. We have to get back to Powers, to get his list of adopters before he's either rescued by his men or killed by whoever's doing the shooting."

"I'm with you," Shannon promised. "But I don't think I'm much good for fighting right now."

"You can leave that part to me. Just stick close, and I *will* get you out of this—I swear it."

"We'll both get out of this," she assured him, though she was all too aware she had no way to guarantee it.

He paused and turned to look at her, his eyes intensely focused. "That's what I intend. But if it doesn't happen, Shannon, if for any reason I don't make it, promise me you'll see to Amber's future. That you'll do whatever's best for her, even if that means raising her yourself."

Shannon's knee-jerk reaction was to swear that she would drag him out, would swim away with him if need be, to keep them both alive. But she knew, they both knew, that anything could happen, even to those fighting on the side of right.

So she looked up at him and nodded, her voice solemn as a vow. "For you, Rafe, yes, I'll do it. If that's what it comes to."

He leaned down to kiss her, a kiss quick as a stroke

of lightning, and just as devastating, as searing in its heat. Then he turned and hurried away, forcing her to follow, to keep up with her heart.

RAFE FOUND POWERS in the galley, still unconscious, and still—thank God—alone.

Kneeling, he shook the man and repeatedly called his name.

When there was no response, Shannon asked, "Are you sure he's breathing?"

Rafe checked quickly, his own breath held until he felt a puff of humid air from Powers's nostrils, then a strong pulse when he checked the carotid artery. "He's alive. Can you get some water? Maybe that'll wake him."

Nodding, Shannon opened a cabinet and took out a glass, her one-handed movements clumsy as she tried to protect her broken fingers. As she set it down so she could turn on the faucet, she cried out a warning, then ducked behind the counter as a thin man wearing a camo hood over ninja-black clothes staggered into the room.

Rafe swiftly came to his feet, drawing his gun in one seamless motion. He nearly blew away the newcomer before he saw that the man's raised hands were empty.

"Don't shoot, Rafe. It's me!"

"What the hell?" Rafe demanded, his pistol still aimed at the man's chest. "You bastard! You're one of the guys who tried to kill us at the motel. One of the men who shot my brother-in-law."

"It's *me*," the man insisted, pulling off the hood that hid his face to reveal the supposedly dead Garrett, his pale face streaked with anguished tears. "It's always been me, from the start."

Shannon poked her head out, staring.

"What the hell's that supposed to mean?" Rafe asked.

Two more hooded men stepped in behind him, both carrying AK-47s. Leaving his face covered, the bulkier of the two said, "I'm Zero, and you'd better listen, Ranger. Because your sister's scum-sucking husband's got somethin' he wants to get off his chest."

THE INTRUDERS HAD GIVEN HER one look and then dismissed her, judging her no threat. *Mis*judging her, Shannon thought, because though she might be both unarmed and injured, the adrenaline coursing through her body was quickly restoring her to life.

Still reeling from her escape and her unexpected reunion with Rafe, she couldn't believe Garrett was there with them, instead of lying dead from the gunshot wounds he had reportedly received at the hotel. Terrified as he looked, she saw no signs of injury, not the slightest indication he'd been hurt.

"If you're alive," Rafe asked Garrett, "then who the hell was shot in the hotel?"

Zero answered for him. "This douchebag got to one of the weapons you left with him before we could subdue him. He took out one of the best players from our tribe."

He was referring to the game, Shannon realized, to an online team the hackers must have formed. But if Garrett was part of it—whatever "it" was—why had they turned against him?

Rafe nodded to indicate both doorways. "What about the other men onboard? Powers's men."

"Killed two," said Zero with an offhand shrug. "And the others ran off. Powers's crew is none too loyal. They've all abandoned ship." He turned to Garrett.

"Now tell him," he said, as his hooded associate prodded Garrett with his automatic weapon. "Tell Lyons about his sister. About how you got her killed."

"Say that this man's lying, Garrett," Rafe ground out through clenched teeth. "Tell me Shannon wasn't right about you from the start."

"I never meant to get her hurt," Garrett pleaded. "Please, Rafe, you have to believe me. I *loved* Lissa. It was just— It started out as just a job."

"What job?"

"It was a side job. Like I told you, I was moonlighting to make extra money so she could stay home with the baby like we both wanted."

A snatch of conversation floated up through Shannon's memory. Garrett saying something about how the government could learn from the pro who had secured Powers's personal system.

What if he hadn't been complaining but boasting about his own prowess? About a system so secure, even its creator had difficulty hacking into it?

Climbing to her feet, she said, "Garrett was the one. The one who locked down Powers's website and his system."

"Did you know what Powers was doing?" Rafe asked, his voice a threatening growl. "Did you have any idea what kind of business you were protecting?"

"Not at first," Garrett assured him. "But then, when I found out…"

"When you found out, you had an obligation to report it," Shannon accused, and Garrett shook his head wildly.

"No! I knew he'd kill me. Or have one of his goons do it. Besides, I couldn't prove I didn't know what he was doing with those surveys from the start, and when

I confronted him, Powers swore he'd implicate me as a fully participating partner."

In two steps Rafe closed in, towering over Garrett, who shrank away. "So what did you do then? What did you do to get my sister killed and your own daughter stolen?"

Garrett lowered his head. "I was in an impossible situation."

"What did you do, worm?" Rafe asked.

"Tell him!" Zero ordered, and the man holding the AK-47 squeezed off a single round.

Garrett went down, howling with agony as he fought to stanch the blood pouring from a wound that went straight through his thigh.

A wound that gushed a bright red arterial flow.

"Hold it," Rafe commanded, his pistol pointed at the shooter's head.

"Rafe, he's going to bleed out," Shannon warned. "We have to bandage him fast, or he'll—"

"Tell me," Rafe repeated, his gaze boring into Garrett's.

"I tried blackmailing him. I tried," Garrett answered in a rush as his face contorted with pain. "But my partner, Angel, must have double-crossed me. He thought I didn't know, that I'd never figure it out, but—"

"Angel told Powers about Lissa," Zero explained. "Told him killing her would scare Garrett into shutting his mouth, since he wouldn't be able to say a word without implicating himself."

"So they murdered Lissa without your knowledge or approval?" Rafe asked Garrett.

"Yes," Garrett answered weakly. "I swear, I would never— I never approved of any of those women's murders."

"You kept your mouth shut about it for weeks, scumbag," Zero accused, "while you were trying to shake down Powers—and they were killing other women."

Seeing the glassiness of Garrett's eyes, Shannon opened cabinets until she found some towels. Disgusted as she was by his admissions, it wasn't up to her to make the final judgment on whether he deserved to die.

"Here," she told Garrett. "Wrap your leg in these and apply firm pressure."

"So where do you two come in?" Rafe demanded of Zero and his silent—and apparently trigger-happy—partner. "Why have you been chasing us?"

"Garrett brought us into this. Asked for our help after you decided to go after Powers," Zero explained. "And we were cool with that. More than cool, 'cuz of what happened to our friend's old lady. But only because we didn't know what this weak son of a bitch and Angel did, helping Powers kill so many women."

For the first time the hooded shooter spoke—in a voice as unmistakably feminine as it was full of rage. "Perfectly innocent pregnant women who'd never hurt a soul in their lives."

"But you're criminals, all of you," Garrett accused. "Both you *and* your brother, Circe."

The woman's automatic rifle swung toward Garrett's head.

"Stop!" Rafe shouted, but it was too late. Circe's AK-47 barked twice, and Garrett slumped, bleeding from a pair of holes drilled through his skull.

Hopelessly outmatched, with both Zero's and Circe's more powerful weapons pointed at him, Rafe glared at the hackers. "He wasn't yours to punish. Wasn't yours to kill."

"He broke our code," Circe said, "the faithless swine."

"We might be criminals, like he said," Zero told them. "But we're not lawless. And Garrett was one of us. He swore to our code."

"First item on it, 'Harm no innocents,'" said Circe. "We don't do it, and we don't help cover it up, either. Our associates saw to Angel yesterday—and now Garrett has paid the price, as well. And the man you killed at the motel—" Her gaze cut to Shannon. "We know you had no idea what was going on—which means we'll be leaving—as soon as we take out one last piece of trash."

With that, she swung her gun toward Dominic Powers, who had finally roused enough to realize the mortal danger he was in. "No, please. I—I can pay you. All of you, I swear it!"

"Garrett wasn't yours to kill," Rafe repeated, and though Zero still kept a gun on his chest, he stepped in front of Circe's weapon. "And Powers isn't, either. He belongs to me."

"No, Rafe. Move!" Shannon cried out. It was true that without Powers, she and Rafe might never find the adopters' names and their locations. But without Rafe… She couldn't bear to think it.

"Listen to him." Powers attempted to rise up on his knees, to hide behind the Ranger's strong legs. "Please! For the love of God, just listen!"

At the same moment Circe warned, "I don't take orders from you, *Captain* Lyons. I'm no man's soldier, and no army's. Now step aside, or you'll die, too."

"You can't!" Shannon shouted. "He's an innocent in this, too. He only wants to save his niece and the other babies." She moved closer, challenging the female hacker, betting her life that Circe's code wouldn't allow her to open fire on an unarmed woman who had committed no crime.

"What about you?" Zero asked Shannon. "What's in this for you?"

"Justice," she answered simply, understanding that her willingness to pursue it at all costs had been her father's true legacy. A legacy not necessarily defined by any rank or badge. "And I can tell you that to find any of those babies, we need Powers alive."

She and Rafe stared down the well-armed hackers, until finally the hooded pair exchanged glances.

Circe nodded at them. "You're right, Lyons," she said coolly. "You're the one with the blood claim here, so we'll leave the slime for you to deal with."

Both hackers backed out through the doorway, and in a moment Shannon heard their receding footsteps.

Blowing out a long breath, she glanced toward Garrett's body lying in a pool of his own blood, a death of his own making. "Oh, Garrett, I was so hoping I was wrong about you."

"That's another on your account, Powers," Rafe said as he hauled the struggling attorney to his feet. "Now it's time to pay up."

Shannon raised an eyebrow at the man who'd ordered her killed. He looked frightened now, pathetic, with his damp clothes reeking of urine. But in spite of what he'd done to her, she only wanted his answers, not his suffering.

"Your client lists aren't on the computer, are they?" she asked. "So tell us, where's the ledger? The ledger with their names."

Chapter Twenty-One

Ruthless as he was when it came to ordering the deaths of others, Powers had no backbone with his own life on the line. With very little prodding, he led them to the master stateroom and gave them the combination to his vault. Rafe held their prisoner at gunpoint, watching carefully as Shannon turned the dial.

"There, that's it," she said once she had opened the heavy steel door. Inside they found a large amount of cash, an envelope filled with loose diamonds, and another containing a small ledger with names, dates and locations.

"Please," Powers said, as he went to his knees before Rafe. "I've given you everything you wanted. Now please, just let me go. I'll never do anything like this again. I swear it."

With Lissa flashing through his mind, Rafe kicked Powers hard in the ribs, kicked him until he went down sobbing, curling into a fetal ball. Rafe would have gone on kicking, or he might have hauled the bastard to his feet and beaten the unarmed man to death, if it hadn't been for Shannon shouting, "No! Rafe! Please don't do this. Let him live to stand trial, so the other murdered women's families can confront him. So his first and second wives' families can get answers."

Feeling adrift from his true nature, he jerked his gaze to her face, so beautiful and battered. A face that anchored his soul despite the storms that raged both outside and within his heart.

"You're right," he admitted, fighting back the images of the thousand savage deaths he had imagined for his captive. But it was one thing to kill out of necessity, in the heat of battle. Another completely to murder a helpless captive—no matter how deserving—in cold blood.

Instead Rafe turned his attention to the ledger, flipping through the pages until he found his sister's name, linked to a couple with an address in Beverly Hills, California.

They had named the baby Zinnia, the healthy infant they had bought, an infant for whom the father—an actor whose name Rafe recognized from a string of eighties action movies—had paid an obscene premium on the chance that she might have his wife's green eyes.

"*Lissa's* green eyes," Rafe hissed as fresh heat seared his own. "And her baby's name is *Amber. Amber Lee Smith,* not something off a damned seed packet."

Shannon came up behind him and laid her hand gently on his shoulder. "Rafe, please, if you ever want to see Amber, to hold Lissa's child in your arms, we can't stay here waiting for Powers's thugs to regroup. What we *can* do is get him out of here to a safe place where we can cuff him, then give the authorities his location."

"You can take him in yourself," Rafe said. "Get the credit for bringing down Dominic Powers's empire."

"Won't do me any good without that book in your hands."

As thunder pealed outside, Rafe managed a slight

smile and offered her Powers's pistol, which he pulled
from his waistband. "Then I guess you'd better come
along with me, sugar—that is, if you're still willing."

She nodded, her gaze locking with his. "Are you
kidding, cowboy? I wouldn't miss this part for the
world."

THEY STARTED DOWN THE GANGPLANK, their heads
ducked against the driving rain as they moved out single
file.

Shannon prodded Powers, who was walking ahead of
her, while Rafe walked in front, his weapon drawn and
ready to blaze a path for them if need be. Wind gusted
off the water's surface, blowing stinging salt spray into
their eyes.

That was when it happened. With Rafe only a step or
two from the pier, sound burst through the darkness—
five thunderclaps in quick succession. Gunshots, and
then a pair of heavy splashes as first Powers and then
Rafe fell, rolling into the churning water as Shannon
fired in the direction of the muzzle flash.

Maybe the shooter hadn't seen her walking behind
the larger men, or she might have died that night. Instead
she shot at the muscular silhouette until Red Beard collapsed onto the wet dock in an unmoving heap.

"Rafe!" she screamed, on her knees at once and looking for him in the wild water. In the darkness she spotted
what might have been a lifeless man's back floating
among the waves, but there was no way she could reach
it, or know whether it was Rafe or Powers who was so
quickly swept away.

Grabbing the precious ledger, which Rafe had
dropped only inches from the pier's edge, Shannon
raced back aboard the yacht, where she took both a

cell phone and a flashlight from one of the men killed by the hackers.

Rushing back outside, she kept repeating, "No, Rafe, no, please," pain jolting through her body with each step and hot tears sliding down her face.

By the time she returned there was nothing to be seen. Nothing at all in evidence except the lifeless hulk of Red Beard's body—she couldn't believe he had accidentally killed his master along with taking down Rafe—and swiftly churning dark waves she knew would quickly pull her under if she tried to fight them.

Still, she might have attempted it, despite her injuries, even though she couldn't have pulled out a man Rafe's size on her best day. Then she remembered the promise she had made him, the vow he'd pulled from her not a half hour earlier.

If for any reason I don't make it, promise me you'll see to Amber's future. That you'll do whatever's best for her, even if that means raising her yourself.

Finally Shannon switched off the flashlight, plunging both her heart and soul into the blackest night. After dialing 9-1-1 and anonymously reporting shots fired and two men in the water, she forced herself to turn away from Rafe. Away from the man she loved and toward a very different future…a future she would never have imagined before he'd grabbed her off that Tampa street on a day that felt as if it had unfolded a hundred years ago.

The Isle of Azul,
French Polynesia
One hundred days after…

WITH NOTHING BUT MOONLIGHT and the ghost of her lost hope to guide her, Shannon walked the island's windward side, where the South Pacific breezes stirred the white sand and troubled the inland emerald jungle to her right.

She was troubled here, too, reminded, by the glittering waves of an ocean a half a world away, of a night when she had made a promise that had sent her on the run. Of a nightmare where she had lost the man who lived in her dreams, the man her sleeping self still believed too raw, too powerful and too commanding to have succumbed to either storm or bullets.

Reality stirred in the form of Amber, nestling closer in the sling that Shannon wore against her chest. Shushing the infant, she stroked the silky-soft head, unable to imagine that in the "real world," the world she had abandoned, she had no legal right to the beautiful, healthy child her heart and soul had instantly claimed as her own.

But it was true. She had no status. No real right, except her sacred vow to a doomed Ranger, to the baby that Everett and Maddi Worth (or *Worth-less,* as Shannon had mentally rechristened the couple) had given up without a whimper in exchange for Shannon's promise not to leak the story to the media.

As if she cared one whit about the idiot actor and his wife, a half-looped nitwit who had seemed more interested in playing with a tiny white stuffed animal than saying goodbye to the child she'd been raising as her daughter. All Shannon cared about was Amber, the sweetly cheerful infant who had become her life.

But not quite *all* her life, because she had spent the past months working tirelessly, using the uneasy alliance she'd forged with Circe and Zero to feed information to her brother, to make certain every one of the babies

Powers had stolen received the happy ending he or she deserved.

"And this will have to do for ours," she murmured to the sleeping baby as the soft breeze ruffled the blue sarong tied at her own hips.

She tried to convince herself that she could be happy living in exile with the help of the money and the diamonds she had taken from the vault on Powers's yacht. With the rest of Powers's fortune distributed among the families of his victims, she turned her thoughts to her own future, a future she had decided to spend using her talents playing Robin Hood to help other bereft families, those whose children had been spirited out of the United States by noncustodial, foreign-born parents.

So she had a family, in the form of Amber, a purpose, in the guise of her new mission, even a paradise, in this beautiful island near Tahiti. If it wasn't all her broken heart had ever wanted, it was more than many people got.

More than...

She turned toward a sound, the sound of swift-approaching footsteps. Cursing herself for growing complacent in the safety of this isolated haven, she scanned the beach but saw nothing.

Sensing her new mother's mood, Amber started, her sharp cry spurring Shannon into running—running for the beachside bungalow where she had a gun hidden.

"Don't move," called a deep voice.

A voice that froze her in her tracks.

A voice that had her heart stuttering, her breath hitching in her lungs.

A voice out of her dreams.

"Do you have *any* idea," Rafe asked, his words a shimmer of emotion, "how long and hard I've been looking for you? How the thought of finding you, of finding both of you, was the only thing that kept me going? That helped me survive?"

"This isn't real," Shannon whispered, not daring to turn toward him. Not wanting to face the heartbreak of an empty beach, another empty night...

His hand settled on her shoulders like a benediction, so warm, so real, so solid, that she knew even before she turned to kiss him...

...that this Ranger, the lost Ranger she had grieved for, finally and forever had her dead to rights.

* * * * *

Available July 12, 2011

#1287 BY ORDER OF THE PRINCE
Cowboys Royale
Carla Cassidy

#1288 RUSTLED
Whitehorse, Montana: Chisholm Cattle Company
B.J. Daniels

#1289 COWBOY FEVER
Sons of Troy Ledger
Joanna Wayne

#1290 HER STOLEN SON
Guardian Angel Investigations: Lost and Found
Rita Herron

#1291 BAYOU BODYGUARD
Jana DeLeon

#1292 DEAL BREAKER
The McKenna Legacy
Patricia Rosemoor

HICNM0611

REQUEST YOUR FREE BOOKS!
2 FREE NOVELS PLUS 2 FREE GIFTS!

Harlequin®

INTRIGUE®

BREATHTAKING ROMANTIC SUSPENSE

YES! Please send me 2 FREE Harlequin Intrigue® novels and my 2 FREE gifts (gifts are worth about $10). After receiving them, if I don't wish to receive any more books, I can return the shipping statement marked "cancel." If I don't cancel, I will receive 6 brand-new novels every month and be billed just $4.24 per book in the U.S. or $4.99 per book in Canada. That's a saving of at least 15% off the cover price! It's quite a bargain! Shipping and handling is just 50¢ per book in the U.S. and 75¢ per book in Canada.* I understand that accepting the 2 free books and gifts places me under no obligation to buy anything. I can always return a shipment and cancel at any time. Even if I never buy another book, the two free books and gifts are mine to keep forever.

182/382 HDN FC5H

Name	(PLEASE PRINT)
Address	Apt. #
City	State/Prov.	Zip/Postal Code

Signature (if under 18, a parent or guardian must sign)

Mail to the **Reader Service:**
IN U.S.A.: P.O. Box 1867, Buffalo, NY 14240-1867
IN CANADA: P.O. Box 609, Fort Erie, Ontario L2A 5X3

Not valid for current subscribers to Harlequin Intrigue books.

**Are you a subscriber to Harlequin Intrigue books
and want to receive the larger-print edition?
Call 1-800-873-8635 or visit www.ReaderService.com.**

* Terms and prices subject to change without notice. Prices do not include applicable taxes. Sales tax applicable in N.Y. Canadian residents will be charged applicable taxes. Offer not valid in Quebec. This offer is limited to one order per household. All orders subject to credit approval. Credit or debit balances in a customer's account(s) may be offset by any other outstanding balance owed by or to the customer. Please allow 4 to 6 weeks for delivery. Offer available while quantities last.

Your Privacy—The Reader Service is committed to protecting your privacy. Our Privacy Policy is available online at www.ReaderService.com or upon request from the Reader Service.

We make a portion of our mailing list available to reputable third parties that offer products we believe may interest you. If you prefer that we not exchange your name with third parties, or if you wish to clarify or modify your communication preferences, please visit us at www.ReaderService.com/consumerschoice or write to us at Reader Service Preference Service, P.O. Box 9062, Buffalo, NY 14269. Include your complete name and address.

HI11

As the dust settled, Dawson got his first good look at the rustler. A pair of big Montana sky-blue eyes glared up at him from a face framed by blond curls.

A woman rustler?

"You have to let me go," she hollered as the roar of the stampeding cattle died off in the distance.

"So you can finish stealing my cattle? I don't think so." Dawson jerked the woman to her feet.

She reached for the gun strapped to her hip hidden under her long barn jacket.

He grabbed the weapon before she could, his eyes narrowing as he assessed her. "How many others are there?" he demanded, grabbing a fistful of her jacket. "I think you'd better start talking before I tear into you."

She tried to fight him off, but he was on to her tricks and pinned her to the ground. He was suddenly aware of the soft curves beneath the jean jacket she wore under her coat.

"You have to listen to me." She ground out the words from between her gritted teeth. "You have to let me go. If you don't they will come back for me and they will kill you. There are too many of them for you to fight off alone. You won't stand a chance and I don't want your blood on my hands."

"I'm touched by your concern for me. Especially after you just tried to pull a gun on me."

"I wasn't going to shoot you."

Dawson hauled her to her feet and walked her the rest of the way to his horse. Reaching into his saddlebag, he pulled out a length of rope.

"You can't tie me up."

He pulled her hands behind her back and began to tie her wrists together.

"If you let me go, I can keep them from coming back," she said. "You have my word." She let out an unladylike curse. "I'm just trying to save your sorry neck."

"And I'm just going after my cattle."

"Don't you mean your boss's cattle?"

"Those cattle are mine."

"*You're* a Chisholm?"

"Dawson Chisholm. And you are…?"

"Everyone calls me Jinx."

He chuckled. "I can see why."

*Bronco busting, falling in love…it's all in a day's work.
Look for the rest of their story in*

RUSTLED

*Available July 2011 from Harlequin Intrigue
wherever books are sold.*

HIEXP0711R

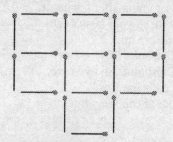